Penguin Books

Jacob's Season

John Hooker was born in New Zealand in
1932. He was educated in Auckland, and
has worked as a public servant, a publisher's
representative and a bookseller. In 1963,
he took up a writing scholarship at a free
university in California, and travelled
extensively in the United States and Europe.
John Hooker now lives in Melbourne
where he works as the Australian editor
for an international publishing company.
He is married and has a son.

John Hooker

Jacob's Season

Penguin Books

Penguin Books Ltd, Harmondsworth,
Middlesex, England
Penguin Books Australia Ltd, Ringwood,
Victoria, Australia

First published by Barrie & Jenkins 1971
Published in Penguin Books 1973
Copyright © John Hooker, 1971

Made and printed in Australia
at The Dominion Press
Blackburn, Victoria

This book is sold subject to the condition
that it shall not, by way of trade or otherwise,
be lent, re-sold, hired out or otherwise
circulated without the publisher's prior
consent in any form of binding or cover other
than that in which it is published and without
a similar condition including this condition
being imposed on the subsequent purchaser

For Jill

I

Across the gully where the pine trees grow, shaking crystal drops that fall upon their twisted feet, stands the house where Jacob Small lives and sleeps. Every blue, cold blue morning, he sees those hairy cliffs of stone, dotted, dripping trees; hears the sound of pipes blown by some early mad-man, the chime of the bell-bird calling through the fragile mist. He, seller of old books (and other things), Jacquie, slenderly snoring, steaming from her nostrils in this frosty morn, and their boy-child, Gideon, starting to sniffle and bawl from his cot. Beads on frames, constructional toys, a plastic duck with hidden squeaker—he knows them not, but cries in his waking for he is cold and Mummy is asleep.

This wooden fortress has seen better days. For in its time of champagne and glittering chandelier, it was the property of monied gentlefolk who made chocolates and fancy bonbons for curly-headed young bucks in bowler hats and their laughing lacy sweethearts. A splendid hall, designed by Mr Boldini, architectural genius of his day and known for his work on several city hostelries. Ceilings of stained glass, a staircase curving from the panelled hall above, banisters of teak imported from Siam, servants' quarters, a marbled fireplace in every room but one, smoking room, dining-hall, vintage wines from France and Spain and Italy lying rack on rack in cool, capacious cellars, garden seats, dovecotes and birdbaths on the lawn. But now, in this time of days and nights, the occupants have been reduced to four: the present owner, Mrs Miffawney, and the Small family, her paying guests. Many bedrooms, then, are bare, unoccupied and unprofitable.

A cold, black, boardinghouse day, and tired timbers creak. Mrs Miffawney's feet pad to the lavatory; balls of fluff on the lino and cigarette butts swelling in the pan. Hair on the soap. Clang. Clang.

Wool in his navel and shrouded uneasily between calico sheets, Jacob yawns and takes a half-smoked fag from the Dewars tray. Through slitty eyes, he considers a sepia of this town in an oval black-wood frame hanging from the scrim, ballooning bulging and billowing from the wall that holds this room together. *From the Hill, Flagstaff, New Zealand.* The peaks rise between the spires and stone embattlements. The winter wind blows and the castle walls shudder. Yellow stains in the basin and last night's cup of tea. GUESTS ARE REQUESTED TO PLEASE PAY

ONE WEEK IN ADVANCE. Blowing smoke from all his nostrils, Jacob regards.

Another daily reminder nearer the grave. Guests are requested to please save their shit for the garden, and oblige. His bones creak and rattle, his knees are wrinkled and his toes are cold. Ho hum, in case of sleep, please use the bed provided. Balls and brass monkeys, he clutches the sheet. The small mountain next to him in bed speaks. Jacquie at her Matins, intoning her early-morning litany. God help this young, softly-feathered bird driven from the mountains. Her thin voice bleats. (Is it Gideon, or is it she?) She peers at her gold wristlet watch he gave her ten thousand years ago. 'Jacob, you will be late. You will be late.'
Jacob will be late.

From the window, the hump of Mount Cargill covered with moss and ice. A fat wood pigeon, green and white-singleted on Jacob's telegraph pole, and there he sees his horse: a big, bony, red, dawn-coloured gelding, standing like some impotent king on his dreadful domain. Ah, the horse is dead, the musterer is asleep. All is long gone; join the Ancient Order of Druids, old time dancing, Jimmy Shand and the leathered hand.

Uncommunicant, he rises, pokes his feet into elastic-sided tartan slippers, skates across the wooden ice-rink and slams the door. Jacquie sinks, and Jacob.

slippered, scarved and dressing-gowned, moves down the varnished corridor, Listerine toothbrush in hand to face yet another day of copper tubes and frigid pipes flushing. A dank morning sperming from dark hills.

Yellow tongue and groove. Tongue and grove? Our child, Gideon, Jacquie dear is howling. He is covered with cold piss, he has lost his woolly Jim Jorgensen. Give him your little tit and comfort him. Frosted glass and old Gillette blades, an Ipana tube like some crusty penis, Odorono, a tortoise-shell hair brush, Chanel talc, a blue duck drowned in the bath, cuticle machinery, Meltonian suede shampoo, his daily inventory. Razor in hand, he sees God's day through the half-opened window, and outside, Mrs Dolan moves, tweed-arsed and boned, carrying shovels of compost for her hibernating bulbs. This is a day of birds' calls and pussy's frozen milk. Next door, Mrs Dolan is early abroad this day, and working in her garden. The mulch drips from her red-boned shovel. Banana skins from old graves, cabbage leaves, rubber-bands, and toenail parings, cottonwool and dobbets of dried blood, orange pips, nutshells and withered poppystalks. The worm wriggles. The back bends and the world is all arse. Cocks and caterpillars, all is going well. All is going well.

Face covered with Palmolive shaving cream, like a bearded king from the Holy Land, Jacob pokes his head out the window where the south wind blows vast from crumbling packs of ice. Smells of frost, horse dung, pine cones, the thin sound of a thousand breakfast-sessions drifting from the tumbled gully below. The silver river Leith, cracked wooden cottages back to back, the pottery factory, great smoking chimneys spouting pieces of soot, floating like huge, black crows, flying, flying, flying. The red gelding has gone.

'Howareya, Mrs Dolan, howareya?'

'Good for me bulbs, Mr Small.'

'What are you using today, Mrs Dolan?'

'Sheeps' dags and mulch. Good for me bulbs and succulents.'

Her arse tightens under the long woollen drawers. Succulents, bulbs and blackbird cack, her swathed body moves across the ruined garden.

'Have you seen me succulents, Mr Small? Mr Small?'

But he has gone to breakfast and a nice hot cup of tea.

Jacquie, poor Jacquie, is crouched in front of the gas fire. Burnt toast and a pot of porridge on the stove, the light of his life, son Gideon, in his skyblue highchair, bulldozing his bent pusher through mudflats of milk and mush. Jacquie, love, he kisses her wee neck, she smelling of baby and last night's talc. Watery blue-eyed and tendrils of yellow hair, she turns, spatulate in hand from the stove.

'I want to leave here, Jacob, I've told you I want to leave.'

'Aw, the house ain't too bad, Jacqueline my love. A bit nippy in the winter, but not too bad.'

'Jacob, you know very well what I mean. This town, this place.' Sniff sniff. 'It's so cold for the baby and there's no future.' Future? Future? What is future? And what is future without Kate? Porridge is marvellous stuff. Trust old Gideon, he knows a thing or two. Fragile canals, and now the milk in gentle rivulets before I start dredging operations. That's it, miniature earthworks. Katie loves porridge too.

'Jacob, don't play with your porridge and listen. We have to get out of this horrible town.'

What town has the chasm, the ice and the pouring rockfall, the silence of the mountain grave where the kea dives and dies? 'Well Jackers, we'll go north soon, I promise you.'

'You've said that for three years now, Jacob.'

His poached egg bleeds on to the plate.

'Not long now, Jackers, not long now.'

She turns and sniffs into the pot of steaming tea.

'Must be off now. Must be off.'

Grab coat. Bonhommie. Kiss neck twice. Kiss Gideon. Skritch, skritch in tummy. Hullo. Goodbye.

'Jacob, don't you want your tea?'

'Aw, bit of a rush.'

And he has gone into his morning.

Outside he stands for a moment, and aches with cold in his groin and ice in his veins. His balls contract. In the town below, dark steam-trains are shunting north to cracked rail ties, to yellow grass and thistledown and cinders burning in the bracken. Above the stone buildings, the day flies high, swept from hills of moraine and glittering ice. Curly chalk clouds racing, a child's day and Jesus is there with all His angels. Tits and knittingneedles, God bless the Scots, pulling their ploughs through fields of stone.

Suddenly a bellbird sings from a leafy tree, and Jacob thinks of Kate again, hums a little tune and goes down to the town.

The south wind doth blow,
And we shall have snow.
What will Jacquie do then,
Poor thing?

2

Comes the sun, the moon is gone and staggering turrets fall. This early day is black and blue, and on the lawn the blackbird hops, listening, listening for the worm. The bell-bird calls, a pigeon creaks across the sky, the cloud is black this day, and black the hills that hold this place and keep it for their own. The town lies silent as the sun comes up from the dark green sea. Hoo hoo, the birds are crying, hoo hoo. Jacob walks slowly down the path past cypresses and dahlia beds, appletrees and concrete gnomes, mapletrees and whiteywoods. Where is the spring and gold, gold, gold?

The road gleams in the southern light shining from the tree, and each side they stand, these old houses, buttressed, bricked and gabled against this wind Jacob knows so well. Pines, macracarpa, sycamore and oak, bluegum and wild broom sweep and bend upon the hill, while on the steps of boardinghouses, knotted hands polish brass in this cold that bursts the lung.

Soon it will snow, and soon the ice will glitter in the

birdbath on the lawn. A time of dark, dark days, and he will have to feed the sparrow when it shivers on the windowsill.

The sun is higher now as Jacob goes down steps and stairs through old willows by cracking chimneys as they smoke this early day.

Now all is sun and cloud as hills heave and colours change. Oh, to climb that winding path twisting on the slope, where in the spring the gorse runs wild and thorns bring blood, red and warm, from the hands that clutch them. Where is that fresh spring day, where lovers play and young thighs run with juice?

Down steep stairs he runs, the earth is sky and the sky is earth this day that laughs and tumbles on this puzzled town. The day is night and the night is day, and all the oaktrees dance and sing, laughing at the cherrytrees withering upon the hill.

But under the smog, the sun has gone and blind stone buildings stand. George Street. God bless the King. The frost is black upon the tar as trolleybuses break the ice and balaclavas squint from steamy windows. The street-lights still shine as Jacob picks his wary way along the frosty flags this dark and early morn. The sun is on the oaktree, but not this stretch of stone. Now troops of thick-legged girls march from windy bus-stops; great-boned skirts and fairisle jumpers. The squat heels tromp and boots crush the beetles; mauve shoes and shopping baskets, the women march to work, fresh from chilly weekends in winter parks, dark cinemas and tired, black Ford V8s.

The city cleaner leans upon his broom and fiddles with his transistor stuck inside his jacket. The knob's in the navel, can't miss the pops and headlines from the news. Get the station, adjust the volume and stick it up your arsehole, the warmest place in town. And good for reception too. Brassbands playing up the rectum, pa pa pa pah pah pah, oh shivering delight. He bends and shoves the broom up the spout in the standard pose. Now he does the drain another way. Upright position. Less fun and games perhaps, but much more penetration. The whipcords take the strain, and a passing bus almost takes him in the khyber as he pokes for cigarette packets and bits of poop that keep Flagstaff from functioning. A Mention in next year's Honours List no doubt.

Jacob, toes turned in upon the curb, thinks and regards. From the depths the band plays on. One of the cheerful brigade, happy in his work and always ready for a chat, but Jacob moves on, hands still in pockets, aching in his quick. Black is the ice up the crack, the smog is blue and he is cold, shooting steam from all his holes.

The shopkeepers sweep, making ready for their day. The wind blows their flapping strides as they cough and gaze upon their handywork. The Bag Shop, Leathergoods. Condoms made from warranted bullockhide, a suitcase for a trip beyond Cargill's frozen mount. Spend the winter in New Caledonia amongst the waving palms and do it in the open. They sweep, they sweep, and the nation speaks. Gooday Harry. Gooday Tom. Howdyabe? Whatsfresh? Dejavaniceweekend? Allmuffledupforthefuckinsun? Haw Haw.

McDee's Saloon. 50,000 HAIRCUTS AT THE OLD PRICE. A packet of fags and a bag of chews to start the day. Jacob stops and goes inside. Aha, behind the counter, the southern princess stands. Neco Snapon Curlers 1s. 9d. She grins and rests her hand upon her hip. Lime Cream & Glycerine, Good for Flaky Scalps. His eyes stare at the goods. June Roses Toilet Soap. Which Twin Has the Toni? She is a fine, big-dugged young woman. I must get on to that before the winter is out. 'Gooday, Cheryl, a nippy morning. Have you got anything I can suck?'
'Hullo, Mr Small.' Her big face grins. 'Have you tried the ju-jubes? Those are very nice.'
Ju-jubes? Well that's probably a start. Put on best smile and stare at them again.
'And a packet of Pall Mall too, if you don't mind.' Her stubby fingers touch his palm as she counts him out the change. She is very cheerful with her jubes bouncing in her bottles. Jacob eyes them through jars of chocolate crunch as they titillate her boyfriend sweater. What else should I buy? Throaties? Bul-

garian Rock? Jaffas? Minties? Nippies? Lemondrops? Mackintoshes' Toffees? She has hocks of finest pork, all rock and cock amongst the chocolate bars. Ho hum, one of these days there should be a time for a spot of slap and tickle and a naughty with this little muscular jube wriggling in the heather. The wind blows beneath the door, no dipping wicks while the breeze is in the southern quarter.

'See you again, Cheryl.'
'Anytime, Mr Small.'
And out he goes.

Tom Aughatane, Jacob's principal and employer, second-hand bookseller and pamphleteer extraordinary, still punctual in his windy twilight years, is also rising like the cold and watery sun. His skin twitches in his sleeping sack as the clock rings. A carved bed-end with a black leather prayerbook, Sankey's hymns and Biblecards in boxes. He fiddles with his hearing-aid, his tweeds tickling his ancient scrotum. Slowly he comes vertical, gathering his stained moneybelt to his navel. Wind the gold watch and snip the chain. His ancient eye observes the day through the window. He goes outside to the lavatory. Mossy path, sleeping silver birch, jumbled heaps of coke and last year's firewood. Heh, heh, a little pee steaming on the corrugated iron. Fumble with the fly, old thumbs. A lovely fresh morning. Pocket billiards for a moment. Pray, do up this button. Then, Police and Firemans Braces stretched over his broad and creaking back, he moves inside to the gas ring to warm the hands and make a pot of tea.

Shop dark, a million forgotten books, pamphlets stock on stack, spiderswebs, immersion heater strung from the light in pot of stew, black onions and catsmeat, high vaulted gallery where only he has been, Aughatane stumbles carefully and looks from the shop window. Without, there is Jacob Small standing and thinking on his day.

He watches Aughatane mouthing through the glass, his rheumy eyes like dogsballs hanging from a string. Christus, Aughie looks crook. Maybe today it will be my shop. The King is dead, long live the King. The door opens and he steps inside.
'Morning, Mr Aughatane. Your jockstrap's showing, sir.'
'Heh?'
Aughatane twists the knob on his hearing-aid for better reception, but his battery is flat. Come in Charlie Able Fox. Come in Charlie Able Fox. Charlie Able Fox? Sunspots, a bad year for communications. 'I said, a nice mild morning, Mr Aughatane.' Throat-mike on, voice at strength nine, but Aughatane is moving away to open his till for business of the day. The kettle steams. Jacob hangs up his coat, inspects the floor for mail, but there is none, and sits down at his desk. Aughatane has gone to the PRIVATE, to recharge his batteries, no doubt.
Awful, dark silence descends, bringing smells of

spotted fly-leaves, dust, wormy piles of *Saturday Evening Posts*, silverfish, broken spines, desiccated glue, cracked leather bindings. Rockfist Rogan fights no more. A rat sniffs in its sleep and a wooden bookshelf creaks. The books are cold. What will I find today? What will I find until I see Kate? Jacob stretches and stands and takes his stock of the shelves by the window. THOS. MCD. AUGHATANE, SECONDHAND BOOKSELLER, backwards. The gold leaf has long, long crumbled. The street outside is empty. Jacob turns, dreaming of young girls riding bicycles, of the farm in the great rocky hinterland where he was born. Red rock, slippery slopes of sheer, caves and miners' graves, the dog shrill-piping-whistled at dawn, called from gullies, sheep on rock-towers, his father's thumbs split by hand-forged tackle snow-country born, the stallion plunging across the splitting ice-fall through the stone-smashing God of floods, the river.

Mr Doomsbury appears from the back of the shop. Mr Aughatane's partner, the old musterer, come down from the mountain, his body all string and binder-twine, blows his nose into an inkwell.
'Gooday, Mr Doomsbury. How's your belly off for fleas?'
'Sheep four feet high they was, and Shorty laid them down gently as a lamb. Forty thousand acres to ride and me big gelding. Sixty year ago.' He stands between the bookshelves like a broken tree.
'Ho hum, Mr Doomsbury, another day another dollar.' Jacob decides to do his traps and moves toward

the shelves. Books my father read. Mrs Craik: *John Halifax, Gentleman*, Ouida: *Held in Bondage*, Kipling: *Plain Tales From the Hills*. 'Have you seen this one, Mr Doomsbury?' But he has gone, to the Library.

Beyond the windows of the shop, the cloud sprawls low on the hill where the grass is wet and the dandelions grow; the hay is cut and the stubble freezes; the tackle rusts and the knife is blunt. Where is the farmer whistling over the hill? Beatrice Harraden: *Ships that Pass in the Night*, Robert Hitchens: *The Garden of Allah*, Jacob turns and wonders what Aughatane has in his back sleeping-room. In the gully, the houses watch, tired-boned and black, stoked with old pokers. Ethel M. Dell: *The Way of an Eagle*.

He looks again out the window and sees a girl passing on the other side. Jacob holds the Mills & Boon romance and dreams. Oh, floats her frock on slender legs as she moves, fragile and tiny-polka-dotted on this morning, pale and beautifully headed, dandling and dallying before misty windows. Touch the glass, tiny fingers, touch, touch. Breathlessly she bends, for she is gently boned with breasts to fit the hand. (He watches spider-like and trembling as she drifts. Heart-stretched, he follows her down George Street.) The sky is blue now, high and up it spirals to the sun where it stays and glitters, O how she dandles floating air as she trips, tiny-steel-heel-tipped and dancing now and again, now now, small and wonderful is her neck,

little ears to bite and nipples soft to kiss and play,
lightly she goes, golden-thighed and tightly waisted,
brightly shining as she moves so light to carry laughing and breathless to fields of freshcut hay, for she is
his, and she is tender, and she will kiss bauble-bright
by bare old oaks and bikes freewheeling through the
traffic where it runs.

She has gone. W. J. Locke: *The Morals of Marcus
Ordeyne.*

3

Bong, bong, the town hall clock strikes five, and Jacob, his pockets stuffed with rare souvenirs of the day (medical brochures, pamphlets, railway time-tables and old travel guides) steps toward the Royal Albert for a brandy-vino to keep the cold away. He stops outside the Pacific Fruit Shop, its windows neon-lit and filled with drumhead cabbages, ivory turnips, hairy red carrots and one small pineapple looking like some shrunken head from far across the sea.

A haul of Aughatane's Biblecards which Jacob has taken on long term:
MORRIS SERIES E 1938
He that hewed timber afore out of thick trees was known to bring it to an excellent work. (Psa. 74)

FLOWERS OF THE GARDEN: BULBICODIUM
Dainty hooped petticoat

Circumcision is nothing, and uncircumcision is nothing, but the keeping of the commandments of God. (I. Corinthians vii, 19)

Too true, too true. The evening sky hangs low as he goes.

Tonight, Flagstaff is an old man's town. Cheap felt hats, fibre attache cases, faces whiskery dishcloth-lined and trembling. Oddly they come and go to the Elder Citizens' Association for a free shit and the Gideons' Bible. Gideon? How is good old Gideon this black and windy night? Twitch no more withered balls. I think I got a cold off that lavatory seat Charlie. Hack hack. Coff coff. The wind blows and Jesus, I am cold and old. Old and cold. Thrombosis? What the King died of? Perhaps I've got it too. Christus-a-um, I feel the arteries hardening. No power in the cable, nails too long and paper in the shoe. Let's go to the Library and read the *History of the Peloponnesian Wars*. Or a man's magazine so I can bite a young thigh. Where's me knobbly cane? The one I cut from an oak tree when I was a strong young lad many years ago and needed no knobbly cane at all.

Jacob goes into the Albert for a drink. O Lord transubstantiate me in a jar of vinegar. Give me a caravan so I can move to warmer parts.

The bar: Tobyjugs, bottles of Long John, Dewars trays, matchbox men, fishes' heads, green liqueurs from the hot West Indies, *Phar Lap*, *Tulloch*, *Sir Dane*, Bobby Brown Welter Weight Champ, the All Blacks' Calendar. SORRY NO CREDIT. The barman farts and serves his clientele.

I'llavafivethistime Sandy if you please. Crook in the gut. Uuuuuuuuuuuuuuuuurrgh. Thought *Goldenage* done well? Bubbling pools of beer and vast teak bars, the glass is full and they dream of the Double while they stand, pockets full of papers, bits of string and forgotten peppermints. Study the form and suck the pencil, the track up north is dry and hard maybe?
I'llavanother Sandy if you don't mind.
Two brandyvinos in his pit, Jacob peers into the Escort Bar and has a little look. The women poke in plastic purses for stained pound-notes, bits of kleenex and pink powderpuffs. Stout and raspberry, vodka and lime, draught bitter, bottles are opened as they chat and drink and rest their breasts upon the bar.
Just a wee one thankyou Fred.
Make mine a five.
I'llavaweespot thankyou Frank.
A halfandhalf will do just fine.
Sameagain thankyou Harry, didn't touch the sides.
Just a drop thankyou Bert.
Teehee Mavis you've got a onetrackmind.

'Hullo, Mr Small, fancy seeing you here.' Cheryl is smiling through bottles of Speights XXXX Ale.
Ook, it is she, the Queen of the Plough and Traction Engine. Grin grin. But not tonight. Save Cheryl for the shortest day. Must see Kate. He turns and has one more for the road.
What's yoor name darling? from the woman by the bar. Furs and hairnet, the thin face nods and dandruff

falls off black-creped shoulders. Mottled legs shift on
redveined feet in ash and toffeepapers. Ech. Ech.
Mousedirt in the missionbox, the hand's on the pump
and God is in his heaven.
It's after six Charlie, after six.
(Ae fond kiss.)
Jacob tosses one more back and disappears into the
dark.
Goonight all. Goonight.

Ho hum,
Katie will chuckle,
And we will fuckle
In a truckle,
Before this night is through,
Hoo, hoo.

Southey Street, where Katie lives. Night as black as
ink, yellow windows shine from terrace houses like
some great, blinded bifocals. Camisoles and underpants, the ghostly washing gleams from fencing-wire
strung from trellises and pergolas. Flap, flap, in the
dark. From the hill he hears the sea, running good
and hard. Across the water lies Peru, mountains of
gold and nipples of steel. Arica, Iquique, Antofagasta,
Santiago, Conception, our man, he is come. Hands
behind the curtains fumble with old news, the tit is
tickled no more. When will Mafeking be relieved?
Jacob stands on the corner before her great, three-
storied mansion that overlooks the Bay. The red velvet
curtains are drawn, but he sees that chink of light.

'Hey Katie,' he bawls. 'Hey Katie, it is your Errol, come in from the night.'

Up goes the double-hung, and there is she. 'Gooday Jacob,' she calls.

The gargoyled door opens.

'Hullo, Katus.'

'Hullo, Jacob. You on your way home?'

'Yeh.' Produces bottle from overcoat. 'Brought you a wee snort to keep the cold away.'

'Have you now?'

She is Irish-built, wrinkled stockings and shiny, dark, mussed-up hair. He steps into the hall. Potstands, tenants' letters, her old tweed coat on a hook behind the door.

'Well,' she says, 'how was the day?'

'Aughie got a hernia stirring his stew.'

'Go on?'

'Uncle Albert's horse has gone randy at the wrong time of year.'

'Go on?'

'Doomo was caught masturbating in the *Illustrated London News*.'

'Go on? I'll just get the containers.'

Katie looks good. Big titties. Mummy, Mummy. Wearing man's shirt, two top buttons undone. Beautiful, gently-rounded country stock. Spuds, trout-streams, post and rail fences and fresh green watercress. This is a girl from the never-never mountains, a dark-haired daughter of the snowy patriarch who wore a jacket of Irish tweed, loved his dogs, braved the gorge, mustered 10,000 sheep, sang soft songs in the mountain crib, shot the sniffing deer, was a man with his wife, held her legs, burned the afterbirth and scrubbed the table, feared the Devil, said his Rosary and drank with the priest.

Katie's room. Cheery fire, coke clinkering in the grate, high vaulted ceilings, round carpet square made from old stockings and scraps of wool, Caltex Road Map of New Zealand. He squints: Flagstaff is missing. Swept away, all swept away to the southern sea where seals bark and bergs of ice a-grumble. Jacob sits on the sofa amid skeins of wool, Dulux Colour Charts and yesterday's provincial papers. Kate comes in with warmed Vegemite jars, puts them down and bending her body, gently touches the crimson coals. Orange fairy sparks splutter and race hand in hand up the black chimney. Zizz, zizz, Dagwood sleeps and all is comfortable. Her strong fingers take the bottle. 'Half or full?'
'Aw, a nice big half will do just fine.'
She sits beside him, sucks her glass and stretches her toes toward the fire. He takes a knittingneedle and tickles her thigh. Faint gnomic scratchings, the fire sparks and gleams. He lifts her dress with the needle.
'Hey, Jacob, have you read the news?'
'Aw, Katus.' More brandyvino to keep the spirits up.
'WANTON DESTRUCTION SAYS MAGISTRATE. A lavatory door and five lavatory seats from a newly erected public convenience and three signs, two of which stated Light No Fires and Burn No Rubbish, were used as fuel for a beach bonfire on the City council Public Domain . . .'

He probes her suspender.

'. . . Mr McGoohan, S.M., described the event as a shocking example of wanton destruction of public property . . .' Katie's hocks are tenderly strung, and soft and round and beautiful.

'. . . the youths were convicted on charges of wilfully destroying three direction signs, five lavatory seats, one lavatory door, two lavatory pans, stoppit, one concrete partition, and a water tap to the total value of £89.14.2.'

'Aw, Katie.'

'Aw, Jacob.'

The news falls upon her breasts, the stockmarket heaves and rises, warm stockinged toes, dress above her knees, she laughs a lovely chuckle to keep the cold away.

'I have a big lust,' Jacob sighs, 'for stockingtops and bottletops and ladies' witches' britches.'

She chuckles again, laughs and breathes. Her news falls all over him as she feeds him wine her lips have touched. She takes his cup, moves herself upon his knee and sucks his honey into her hive, his pressure sup and sap of Spring unfelt since he was a bright young lad lying on a golden pebbled beach, all is sweetness now this darkness night of mid-July. He drains her drinking cup, oh, comes in my mistress from the night, sweet as acorn seeds lying on the grass beneath knotted trees of oak, darkblue eyes and snuggletits, black hair piled high and softly to the touch, buttons opening down her front, mummysbreasts in bed with the blinds pulled down to keep the cold and glittering moon away, hot milk and twilight snug-me-downs, her tongue is tippypink and strong between his teeth. Dark wide eyes to kiss, he dances down her neck like a butterfly, her nape is tendril-sweet, he dreams of soap and bubble baths, talcum on his pillow, she is dark and dewy, full of fun and rich red blood to melt the frost of winter nights, perfumed handkerchiefs, beads and blouses, summer cotton frocks, his heart is high as she sighs and muscles in her thighs where he lies, kisses touches and strokes her sweet and frilly finery, and she laughing holds him there, teasing him softly downed, giving him her mouth now and then, in the twinkling of an eye, long-lashed and dark, as playful as a fairy's touch, her long black hair is unpinned and she smiles, her breasts are soft and sweet to suck her warm white milk, and she gives them laughing tenderly and bends her back from her dazzling petticoat that falls and spreads joyously upon the couch where they lie hand on thigh, whisper and breathe and bite and kiss, limbed and thighed and tangled in her hair, while outside all the feathered twilight birds sing and cry, flying flying flying.

Complete disarray, tangled skeins of wool, fragile straps undone and buttons on the pop. They both grin.
'Jacob, Jacob, my spurting super-boy.'
'Um, um.'
Silence as they warm their feet in the afterglow. The black coal burns.

'How's your sister doing these days?'
Sister? Sister?
'What's her name? Jacqueline?'
Goodgrief.
'Ah, hem haw, justfine, justfine.'
'Must meet her when she's down the street.'
Draw breath, suck in deeply, reach for Pall Mall, play with fire poker. 'Not much chance of that, Katus. She's got this kid, you see. Unmarried mother. Dreadful case. Gang-banged by a bunch of hooligans on St Kilda Beach. Simply turrible, tut tut.'
'Haw, Jacob.'
'Honest Injun.' He yawns and stretches elaborately like a creaking semaphore. Consults watch. 'Look, must be off, time's a-wasting and Tom Cobbler's cold. Heh heh.'
She looks at him. 'Well, if you must, you must.'
Kiss kiss, nuzzle nuzzle, and off he goes.
It is dark and Jacob's day is done, and he goes home between these granulated heaps of stone that once were glittering rococo and gleaming marble, ionic-columned and spreadeagled for the thrusting muscle when this town lay her body upon the hill.

The street is empty but for a coupé, red and charging at the lonely dark. Now the south wind blows across the bloody sea that aches with ice and rock and shivers beneath black-bellied clouds, twisting high upon the hill.

But once, by Christ, this town was Florentine with

breasts so sharply speared they cut the lips that sucked
them. Her fingers gripped the swelling hills that lay
upon her body and tore them open for the sun to
burn them black and gleaming for the ruck of pick
and axe that pierced and broke their shining veins,
while she and all her lovers sang. And once, they say,
lads and lasses ran up the winding towpath, along the
tops of cliffs that fell shouting to the sea, dazzling as it
broke upon the rock that held its million tiny drops
for all the world to see, when all Corinna went a-
maying.

But now this wind blows down dark corridors of brick
and stone, flings the grit into the face that gleams
beneath the lamp and disappears behind the door.

We've left the light on dear,
shines the light behind the door
of frosted glass and tallstemmed yachts that sail
on silver northern seas.
We've jasmin growing in our garden,
the moon is gone, the sky is down tonight.
Shall I cut the only rose
now that winter's come?
No wind nor cloud for me, my dear,
no wind nor cloud for me.
Park your bike upon the porch,
bring some sticks in for the range,
let's make a pot of tea.
No wars for us, no dark invaders,
but this wind from Silver Peaks and Saddle Hill

that blows beneath the door
and scatters ashes on the floor,
that blows the thistle, sycamore and pine
in parks and places, where after dark,
little girls should never go,
where little girls should never go.

The paths are swept. Weeds grow in streetside gardens of catmint, lavender and dead forgetmenots. And from their hillside, the stuccoed houses watch the lights across the bay, shivering in this rocky claw that grips this whimpering windy place, so shagged and bitten to the bone, its dried old marrow cracks and falls in cold winter rains, where it dissolves and flows down ancient pipes and drains for seabirds to feed and suck this wrinkled night. This night, creeping down grainy papered halls of villas, blinded like poor old whores who stand alone in parks of elms and blackened pines.

The trellis falls
the thorn is dead,
and Jacob is alone
on this headland in the south,
where the old and slimy seal
rolls in surf so cold, the rock itself is never still,
but shudders, splits and falls, crying to the birds,
who search for fishes' guts upon the southern sea,
which flows from that vast land of ice and snow,
where fresh green spinnies never grow.

4

Jacquie is in bed, alone and palely loitering.
Who had blue eyes and yellow hair? Genevieve? Guinevere?
Bonhommie at all costs.
'Gooday, Jackers, your prince has come. Ahem.'
'Jacob, where *have* you been?'
Where *have* I been? Can't remember. Think.
'Stocktaking. Never thought the old bastard would let me go.'
A very stout effort.
'What did you have for tea?'
'Pea, pie and sauce. Correction. Pie, pea and sauce. Very nutrifying.'
'You're always stocktaking. You've been stocktaking for bloody months.'
'Well there's lots of stock.' Don't pause, try catalogue technique. 'Comic Section: *Film Fun, Jingles, Tiger Tim, Buck Rogers, Hurricane Hawk, Moon Mullins, Alley Oop, Bat Boy*, um um um.'
'Oh shutup, Jacob, you're simply never home.' Sniff sniff.
'Collected novels of Ouida, the definitive Edgar Rice

Burroughs, hand-tinted folding postcards of Flagstaff Railway Station 1892.' Try attack. 'Well, for Christ-sake imagine a complete set of *Home & Beauty* since 1947.'

'Well if you *are* stocktaking, I'm going to talk to Mr Aughatane, seeing he's not on the phone. Why are you not on the phone? I can't call you during the day, or anything.'

Thankgod, a break, a break.

'Christ, Jackers, you know how mean old Aughie is. Mean as catshit. Just the other day I found a Bandaid among the *National Geographics* and . . .'

'I don't care, I'm going to see Mr Aughatane.'

See Mr Aughatane, *see* Mr Aughatane? Omygod. Bring out battered medical bag and adjust stethoscope.

'Well I wouldn't do that if I were you.'

'Why shouldn't I see him if you *are* stocktaking all hours God made and one more?' The kleenex is pulled from the box.

'He's sick.'

'What's the matter with him? You never told me he's sick.'

'I didn't want to worry you with Gideon and all, but he's *really* sick (don't pause for breath) he wears one of those electro-botanical belts, it cures backache, dyspepsia, gout, nervous nightsweats, and he's got piles, sinusitis, intestinal complications and swelling of the prostate gland . . .'

'Jacob (snarl snarl) where have you BEEN?'

'. . . and the dirty old bastard's gone and got gonor-

rhea, and measles, measles. Think of Gideon. Tsk tsk tsk.'
'Jacob, I can't believe a word you say any more, not a word you say.'
'Aaaw, Jackers.' Christus, where are me bloody fags?
'Look love, I'm desperate for a leak, be back in a jiff.'
He blows kiss from cold palm and makes for the door. Uno momento, aaaaaaark. But she is crying and she is cold.
Down the stairs he slides. A nice cup of tea and a smoke by the kitchen fire.

In the hall below, Jacob peers through the yellow chink in Mrs Miffawney's door. THE LAUGHING CAVALIER grins from her wall. The gas smells and the mint is dead. The boards are loose, and the lino withers on the floor. Pots and pans, a picture of Flagstaff's first cablecar and bowlerhatted gentlemen, handtwisted teacosy, willowpatterned plates in racks, pottedferns and wizened cacti in plastic pots. Yellow leaves crawl up thin green bottles and climb toward the moon, the floor is wet and smells of ancient feet. DOMESNIGHT. Toejam is the order of the day. The sink is full and dishes drown. A fretwork dog, chromium yacht, tomato pepperpot. A brass Buddha sits on the sagging shelf, the lace curtains droop. He squints. A blowfly lays its golden egg on the swollen sheepsheart bleeding on the bench among bits of baconrind and empty packets of Liptons tea. Casseroles and gravyboats, all is going well. All is going well.

'Ahem.' The door creaks. 'Goodevening, Mrs M. You wouldn't happen to have a spare cigarette, would you?'

Mrs Miffawney looks toward the door. 'You haven't paid your rent lately, Mr Small.'

Rent? Rent? What is rent? Money paid in kind, tsk tsk.

'Well, hem haw, it's me employer, Mr Aughatane. He's in severe financial difficulties y'know.'

She looks.

'If you happened to have studied the Financial Page of the *Flagstaff Daily Times*, you may have noticed that secondhand postcards have taken the plunge.'

She looks.

Swing Wall Street black bag and adjust narrow-brimmed hat, flick cigar ash from Burberry coat.

'A slight setback on the part of secondhand books and pamphlets, Mrs M. The business is basically sound, but as I say, a slight setback.' Hoo hah. The Rockies may tumble, Gibraltar may crumble, they're only made of clay, yeah, yeah, yeah.

She looks.

Try empty fruitbarrow act.

'Deadburb? Have me pin. Ha ha.'

Her bootbutton eyes narrow to mere steely slits. 'Tomorrow's your last day, Mr Small.'

'But Mrs M, what about me child? Gideon. Named after the greatest junglefighter of them all. Saved Burma, the Empire, the whole world.' He slithers down the door. 'What about HIM . . . and my wife . . . a second mother-to-be?'

'I didn't know she'd fallen again.'
'Oh aye she has and all (beatific smile) she's carrying me own seed. Another little Small is coming through the portals.'
Tears are not far away, sniff sniff.
'Tomorrow's your last day. And close the door, my guineapigs are catching a chill.'
Jacob disappears, and Mrs Miffawney sinks back to open up her readingmatter. Disgusting, disgusting, they always have their hands in each other's pockets, got a bad migraine too and all fluttery in the stomach, a silent tear for SIX KITTENS ABANDONED ON MAIN SOUTH ROAD, such people should be horse-whipped, I must say a prayer for Mrs Dolan with nodules in her fallopians, it makes you think everything is just around the corner.

HE OFTEN BATHED THEIR BABY

and I must have faith, shall I ask the Vicar?

CROCHETED TRAYCLOTH

what would heaven be without animals? Beverly Nichols says there are cats in heaven

GLAMOROUS MINCE

some flowers for Mrs Dolan and some mags to pass the time, you always learn something from *Woman's Own*.

PROBLEM CLINGER

the Lord gave and the Lord hath taken away.

Outside, full of glum, Jacob stands once more in his baronial hall. No servants carousing in their quarters, but smells of boiled marrow and turnip-pee, fish-head soup and brusselsprouts. He opens the door and steps upon the wormy wooden porch, sees a yesterday's fag and applies the match, gasps and stubs it out on her prize cactusplant. Bitchface, mobiletwat, turdpot, bastardcunt, flagellations with stockingsfull of hot shit. He eyes the moon and steps inside again, carefully inspects the rack for a communication which might bear his name. A lone traveller's card: *McGillicudie Bros. Commercial Cleaners. Ph. 35-353 Day or Night. Dirt is Our Specialty.* For Jacob, nothing. He goes again into this medieval night, undoes his zip and pisses expertly on her hydrangeas, steps inside and creeps upstairs to bed.

Jacob listens: Gideon is breathing. Full of yawns, he undresses and climbs into his Woolworths striped pyjamas. *I Was a Fugitive From a Chain Gang.* Paul Muni grimace, but Jacquie is asleep. He climbs in and wraps his body around her wee warm arse. 'Hey, Jackers, Mrs M's a nice old thing, we had such a lovely talk.' Tickle-ickle. 'She's going to lend you her *Woman's Own*s, when she's read them of course, and her Parish mags, and her knitting patterns. Little cardies for Gideon hum hum . . .'
Jacquie opens one blue eye.
'And do you know what I did today? Sold a complete set of Raphael Sabatini. CAPTAIN BLOOD. Roar roar.'
She is warm.
'Hey, Jackers?' He slides his leg between her knees. 'Jackers?' She tiny-moves.

'Please?'
Finger in her bellybutton. Tweek tweek.
'Pls?'
Little ear kisses.
'Ps?'
She turns to him.
'Yum yum.'
Their bed is warm and dark, hidden from the southern moon, and she half-sleeping turns to him and kisses, and he half-sleeping dreams of loving her in parks and under trees before this winter came.

Together, then, they walked the unsure path where thistles blew; ruffled thrushes' feathers in gardens sleeping spindthrift down and racing was his heart in that change of season. The hills were purple-plum and small white horses danced, billowed breathlessly her dress and caught his heart as they clung through silver birches into crickets' songs and leaves of gold away from the town and the traffic's run.

Lifted were their hearts, the sky was blue and swinging overhead and down it went below the hill and above again where white clouds bunched and bundled, hand in hand they flew above the town, beyond red brick and roofs that glittered, and childs' cries, for they were wild birds, winging singing caught and spun as spiders' webs, spinning green and gold above the clock tower as it chimed the hour of wild crushed strawberries, and kisses blown from soft cool hands held together.

Sherry-golden was that day, black-birded and wildberried in leaves that fell and spun in wind-blown hair that fell and kissed in his face. The oaktree laughed as they fell and clambered into beds of pine-needles, sharp and dark as blackberry wine, drawn from casks blue and green as roots that twined and bound that sweet pilgrimage.

Mossy were the banks then, for summer had gone, and tumbled all the stones, grey-hued and speckled with seeds; and as they came, sparrows laughed and rose, winnowed and willowing on the breeze as it raced, hand on knee and trembling from pines and sycamores that bent and blew, silverdomed, topped and treed, greendark and sighing on that certain day of joy.

Silently they sat, each other close and breathing thigh on thigh; her hands were sweet and silken was her body, sweetly breasted and kissed by his glances; sun and light so was she, tenderly nippled and slender as a breeze's bough as they kissed and felt and tongued soft-tipped tender, he kissing her eyes and she his, blinded by the moment as she snuggled and touched, her hands telling his what to do, where they were and why; God, he loved as she lay and fondled his to pound and break, sweet was her back on his hands through the silk, and how he touched everything of hers, and she of his, he of hers and she of his, that day.

That day of the bird, whose tiny claws tore the paper leaves of a season dying.

Beyond the hill, the snow was falling in black crevices

of rock. Apples, strawberries, pears and plums,
cherries, apricots and peaches had all been harvested,
stowed and stored. Then the hawk flew high alone
above the wrinkled river, and from the south it came,
that windy change of season, creeping into city streets
and backyard lots to grip the head and feet and close
like steel that held fast the sniffing rabbit in the trap.
From the tree, they heard the morepork's cry, and
from the grave, twa corbies maned, cree cree in the
wind that blew and held its steady course, in that wind
that blew and held its steady course.

Sweet Jacqueline, Jacob dreams.
Jacqueline, voulez-vous coucher avec moi?
Um.
Voulez-vous?
Ziz
zz
z.

The Saturday rain has gone and the day is great. The wind is from the south, and Jacob sits upon his hill, watching butterflies, cherry trees and ragwort racing down tumbling slopes headlong for the bay. The grass is wet and these hills lie silently like old crones, their dresses hitched above their knees, sleeping in the sun.

He blows the time on a dandelion, ten o'clock and away they go, floating down silverdown to the gully where old totaras grow and bush rats run amongst old stumps of long forgotten fires that burned so long ago he scarcely can remember, for he was childish then, before this place was stumped and strained and beaten to the quick by the tackle rusting in the shed beyond that grove of pines.

The wind is in the grass this day and crickets sing and gorse seeds pop as the bird flies high and hovers, hovers, in this morning of fires burning on the hill. The cliffs of stone are black and grey and beautiful, the moss is green and brown, and it too shivers in this breeze that blows the leaves of Jacob's season. He picks a buttercup and holds it to his chin, while groundlarks rise and butterflies race and float around battered stumps high upon the hill, where brown moths fly and yellow daisies grow amongst the gorse, in this summer-winter day.

Jacob sucks a straw and dreams of bubblepipes, and there among the glistening trees, he thinks he sees the yellow breasted tit? the silver eye? or did he hear the warbler call? The sky is gold and gentle breezes blow around these bald old hills, and in the gullies seabirds gather to pick the bones, where tangled harrows lie beside the discs that slice the breast red and deep. But soon the rain will fall again and blood will flow from the wound and down the stream moving to the southern sea to stain the feathers of the dusky plover and the giant albatross.

Through the rocks the lizard runs green and striped, so quick is he, so quick that he escapes Jacob's eye as it wanders up the hill and he dreams of secret paths overgrown so long ago the farmer has forgotten. Deep is the pool in the limestone pit, the buckets have all been taken and the chain is snapped. Now the wind carves the stone that lies upon the hill, flaked and chiselled like an ancient artefact thrown up from a dark and bitter sea.

Sing wires sing,
the ryegrass weeps tears for a young man's shoulder.
Californian thistles bloom sweet and green by the

house of stone. The seed is damp and lost its sting, the dragonfly soon will die and leave this place for the bluebottle to suck and lay its egg in the carcass of the sheep tangled in the wire. Three old houses stand by the pit where the fantail, the robin and the thrush poke for seed among the twisted rails and broken springs. The harbour gleams, the rock is fall, and the duck from paradise seeks the long and cold lagoon in the rush and brake where scallop shells and girdled winkles lie in empty rows and soon will disappear next high spring tide.
And green the rushes grow,
and green the rushes grow.

Brown ducks rise and shining cuckoos call, silver silver, in this southern place, where kale and turnip sprout on steep green slopes down down toward the town that breathes heavily in its bed. The southern wind is colder now, and ruined poplars weep their gold into frothing streams that soon will choke with ice. The earth is damp and no lovers play in the leaves and fragile sticks by groves of oaks that dazzle dazzle. The veins are hard and the blood turns black as it drips from the dying limb. The bridge is down and drowns in watercress. The bee still sucks, but the bloom is dead. The cold is in Jacob's bones as he rises to his feet and trundles down the hill to his doomy nest.

Whistling his favourite tuneless tune, Gorman makes his way up the path to Mrs Miffawney's house, mounts

the marble steps, opens the door and climbs upstairs.
Knock knock. Big and heavy, he waits.
'Hullo, Gorman.' Jacquie is at the door, blond and seeing him, decides to smile.
'Good morning, Jacqueline. Where's Jacob today?'
'Out.'
'Out?'
'Out.'
'Well,' he speaks, 'I just thought I'd drop by if I was passing.' He looks at her, thoughtful. 'You're looking good Jacqueline, and it's only early in the day.'
'Why, thank you, Gorman' (she smiles again) 'you can come in and wait by the fire, but I don't suppose he'll be in for hours.'
The clock ticks and Gorman is in her snug keep. Gideon in Moses basket peacefully sleeps. The windows steam.
'He's got big, hasn't he?' Gorman intones.
'Who?'
'Gideon.'
'Aye, he's got big. Do you want a sherry while you wait?'
Gorman looks up. 'I wouldn't say no.'
He brings out his Dutch Mixture and stuffs his pipe, watches her as she bends into the baroque sideboard for a fresh bottle. 'How long is he going to be?'
'Who?'
'Jacob.'
'Oh Christ, I don't know. He's never home.'
Gorman pulls at his beard and looks at her back as she

comes up from the cupboard. Cardigan on back-to-front and buttoned down her slender spine. Jacquie tips the bottle and the amber liquid flows. Gorman sucks his glass, puffs his cherrywood and considers through his hornrimmed glasses.
'You're a fine lass, Jacqueline.' He lays a heavy, careful hand on her arm. 'I don't think he deserves you altogether.'
'Who?'
'Jacob, Jacob.' He grips his pipe impatiently between his big teeth. She sticks her breasts out through her jumper.
'Well, I wouldn't say that, but he is a trial you know.'
She moves over and sits beside him on the sofa, her dress above her knees. Gorman takes a quick look and puffs.
'He's wasting his talents, Jacqueline.'
'Who?'
'Jacob.' Puff puff.
She sighs, stretches her arm and takes the neck of the bottle 'Here, have another sherry.' She pours, the bottle gently clicking against his glass.
'What does he do in that book shop all day?'
'Your beard's quite grown, Gorman. Yes. Now Essau was an hairy man . . .'
'What?'
'Nothing. What does he do all day. Ha, you tell me.'
'Tsk tsk.' Puff. 'Well, I can't understand it.' (He sneaks a look at her knees.) 'He's intelligent, educated, my best friend, intelligent.' Puff. (Her suspender

now.) 'Do you want me to have a word with him? As his best friend?'
'Oh, it'll do no good. I don't get down town much anyway.'
Sniff.
Outside the window, Jacob's wood pigeon waits, fat and green, upon his post.
'Gorman?'
'Yes?'
'Do you think I'm still attractive?'
His deep chest breathes. 'You know that for years, er ah, for years . . .' Puff.
'I'm not *that* old Gorman.'
'No no no . . . ever since I first met you . . . ah.'
'In fact you want to go to bed with me, don't you, Gorman?'
His hands clutch the cherrywood. 'Well, nowthatyoucometomentionit.'
He plunges in for more tobacco.
'For God's sake, Gorman, stop playing with the bloody pipe, when you can play with me instead.'
'Playwithyou? Playwithyou?'
She sips her sherry, sucks a strand of hair, hiccups tinily and stretches out her limbs. 'Nobody loves me, Gorman. I'm stuck in this bloody house day in day out and nobody loves me.'
He ignites a trembling wooden match. 'That's justnot true Jacqueline . . . for years and years.' He sticks his pipe into his mouth and lays his hand upon her knee. Suddenly a creak on the stairs, an opening door, and Jacob stands, breathing cloud, the sounds of birds,

holding wild flowers. 'For thee, Jackers,' he says. 'For thee.'

Jacqueline takes the flowers from him, moves to the kitchen tap, fills her favourite vase with winter water and says nothing.
'How's things, Gorman?' Jacob asks. 'How's the medical world? Got any free bottles of Clement's Tonic, cardboard trusses, Bonnington's Irish Moss made from pectoral oxymel of caragheen found only on the north coast of Ireland?'
Gorman, pipe in hand, composes his reply, but Jacquie, boned and breasted, comes out with her flowers and places them on the dark deal table.
'Look Jackers, I've just dropped in on me way back to town. Great constitutional. Saw a dusky plover and an albatross. Oh Christjesus, a tremendous morning. Great ruined trees and barbedwire entanglements.' (On Mt Cargill's slopes his great red gelding stands and snorts uncertainly.) Gorman probes his pipe, and she bends over his late season flowers, which only crystal moments ago dallied in the wind from low peaks and foggy paths where the grass doth grow.
'Look, Jackers, didn't have the heart to tell you but Aughie wants me back thisarvo for the last of the stocktake (is Katie rising from her bed now?) meanoldbastard (sigh sigh) Scottish secondhand shithead, in the worker's grave I'll be, but look a couple more hours should see me through, ahem.'
She rises from the flowers he has given her. 'Jacob, if you must, you must. But don't be long.'

Gorman brings from his pocket a great metal lighter and applies it to his knotty pipe.
'Look, shan't be late, shan't be late. Have an afternoon drink with Gorms.' (Now Katie is on her way, fresh, perfumed and darkly shining to the park, where the glasshouse gleams, imported cacti grow by the ruined rotunda, where she will stand and hold his hand, hold his hand.)

Then the wind blows the door open and towards it Jacob goes, but he loves his lady of the flowers, and moving forward, kisses her. Kiss kiss. Bugger Aughie. Bugger bugger bugger. Oh sweet Jesus. 'Cheerio, Gorms. Take care of her.'
'What will you eat, Jacob?'
Oh God please give me strength. And he has gone down the stairs into this windy afternoon of trees and wooden pines. His pigeon croons upon its nest, the wattle bends against the window pane, Gideon sniffs and dreams, and Jacquie's blue and yellow flowers breathe and smell beautiful. Gorman, plagued with medical uncertainties, puffs and puffs. She looks at him, sighs, and passes back the bottle.

6

Rain, rain, go away, come back another day.
It falls gently on the Botanical Gardens, where the band is playing in the soundshell by the greenhouse of fricker fretwork and panes of steaming glass. Jacob meanders steadily among weeping elms and sycamore. Hatted and scarved, the afternoon audience stands listening to Old Favourites while wet leaves fall.
Jolly boating weather pya pya pyapyapya pya pya pypyaaa.
The river Leith runs its tiny course between grey walls of slimy, ornamental stone, beneath the narrow wire suspension bridge and over concrete weirs, on its way to the silted, landlocked harbour.
Jacob looks at the dunny water. Where is My Love? Where is she? Ah, there she lies, legs apart and pants showing spreadeagled in a punt on the broad and flowing stream. Spring is come, ha ha, and oak buds pop. Blades flashing, an eight shoots past. Voices drift across the water from the striped marquee on the lawn.
Pya pya pya-pyapya.
Stop poling, Jacob, lie down beside me and recite some pomes by Ella Wheeler Wilcox.

Pong, pong. In the ditch a spotted pisspot clangs. Ha ha Bob a dyrect hit. Goodoh.
Jacob sighs and moves to the ornamental pond where brown ducks paddle and shivering goldfish lie in cold, tentacular weed.
Quack quack. Quack quack. Bumsup. Bumsdown. Bits of bread and a waterworm. Uuuuuuuuuuuuuuuuurgh take it out George. Take it out pulease. The duck might bite your finger.
Pyapya pya pya.
Ewantsitrammedupisarsejackboyfuckingopenendfirst. Haw.
Motorbike boots and bandylegged girls in dufflecoats and mini-skirts.
The cold mouths chomp. Turrible. Turrible. A touch of the birch. Bloody the back and salute the flag.
O Stuart take me, take me to the Edinburgh Festival please. Stirling Castle and wee timorous beasties. Vive l'Ecosse. Vive l'Ecosse. Night must fall and we'll soon be home, tickling each others' tweeds and lumping coal for the fire.

RARE BIRDS. Behind the cage, the lovers talk while the red-plumed parrot springs from swing to swing.
Cockateil. Leptolophus hollandicus. Hullo Cocky. Hullo Cocky.
Lay me down on mossy banks, cinchbelts tangled.
Have a chew?
Ulp, the parrot swore.
Disgusting. Disgusting.
Will the Kiwi lay an egg?

Toffee papers drop into the bed of *phlox drummondi*.
God Save our Gracious Queen, God Save our Noble
Queen. Princess Anne's such a big girl.
The children laugh. Pretty Cocky, pretty Cocky.
Let's go home. Let's. The fire's lit, the soup is on and
the sheets are aired. Comeon Harry, let's. Leeeet's?

Thurnbergia Laurifolia. Heh heh. *Family Acanthaneae. Perennial Climber Native of Malaya.* Aughatane sniffs, bends, and behind his withered hand, spits into the potted palm. Jacob watches him through pyramids of blood and bone. Smells of humus, leafmould and clotted stalks. The old pores sweat in unaccustomed heat. Twisted vines from north of the motorway. Pots and pineapple tops, Aughatane shuffles, pokes his thumbs behind his bracebuckles and peers into the aquarium. A goldfish farts. *Plumbago Capensis.* Potted fern. Hum? The knotty finger is jabbed into tennis-courts of bat's guano drying vast in trays. Outside, falls the rain.

'Gooday, Jacob. Sorry I'm late. Pooh, blood and bone.'
Katie stands beside him like a dark green tree. 'What are you doing behind all this fertiliser?'
'Watching old Aughie.'
'Who?'
'Aughatane.'
'Why?'
'It's the first time I've ever seen him outside his bloody shop. He's a secret botanicalist. He masturbates over nasturtiums when no one's looking.'

'Oh, Jacob.' She takes him by the arm.
Aughatane pokes his face in to the orchids, his braces stretch and his hearing-aid is hooked. Woops. *Acalypha Spiralis? Vriesia Carinata?* His volume is on. PULL BOYS TOGETHER. Ech. Off he sets towards Jacob's machine-gun post of blood and bone, number-nines down the crazy paving, dragging the rare *Aphelandra Tetragona*. He gazes at Jacob with beady bloodshot eye. 'Ech, Mr Small, and your Good Lady? Hum hum.' And from the glasshouse he goes.
' "Your Good Lady?" '
'Ssssssssh. Am conducting a survey of senility in second-hand booksellers over the age of ninety-eight.' Jacob moves stalkily to the window and peers out.

Aughatane is at the Wild Life Cage. DO NOT FEED THE BIRDS AND ANIMALS. Heh, heh, the greatest collection in the Province. Kakarika. *Cyanoramphus auriceps* and red fronted parakeets. He feels in his gaping pockets and pokes his bread through the wire. Monkeys too? He makes an offering. Bluuuuuuuuurt. The old nostrils twitch. Hurriedly Aughatane consults his timepiece, and boots amongst the sycamore seeds, back past the glasshouse he goes.

'*Very* interesting. A unique example of circumlocutory senility.'
'What did he mean by "your Good Lady"?'
'Aaaaaah, the old bugger's mad. Probably thinks you and I are betrothed or something.'
'What would give him that idea?'

'Look, he's mad, mad, mad.'
'Why do you stay with him then?'
'He's teaching me the trade, you see . . .'
'How can he teach you the trade if he's mad?'
'He's not *that* mad. Cunning mad. Foxy mad. Ferrety mad. But every day I pick up something, and his business is a potential goldmine . . . (sigh sigh) . . . look Katus, this is a bloody stupid conversation to have surrounded by hundredweights of blood and bone in the middle of a broken down glasshouse. Let's go down to the Tasman and have a few noshes before six.'

She takes him by the hand as they walk along the narrow path that winds between chilly shrubs and black large-leafed gunneras. 'Come back to my place for sherry and toast and I'll stoke up the fire.'
His threadbare heart pounds. 'Nothing I'd like better, Katus, nothing better (omygod, handsqueeze, fingers entwined) but my sister's kid is ill. Turrible case. The doctor doesn't know what it is . . . spots, stertorous breathing, convulsions, the lot.'
'That's bad, Jacob. I've told you before I want to meet her. Maybe I could help.'
'Help? Help? You couldn't do that. The thing's infectious.'
'What about you then?'
'Aw, I've had every disease under the sun at one time or another. Fit now, of course, but chockful of antibodies I am. Besides I didn't want to tell you this, but Sis is a bit of a nut-case after that beach business . . .'
'What beach business?'

'And she's not my real sister, she's my step-sister by one of my father's previous marriages.'
'Jacob, I've just realised I don't know where you live.'
'Live? Away out at Woodstock. Bloody miles. Little farmlet up in the bush. She's got a few pigs and chooks and I keep an eye on the place. Foot-and-mouth's particularly bad now. Ha ha. Look (thankgod) here's the Tasman. What about a couple of snorts in the cosy back bar?'
In they go.

PRIVATE BAR. Stained glass windows art nouveau, varnished benches and stock-necked women drinking sweet sherry this wet afternoon. The upright piano plays, the banjo plunks and the black bones click.

There they have the time of their life
I saw a man who danced with his wife

The Tasman. Abel found this southern island, covered with strange trees and mountains high with wild blue ice. In sixteen-hundred-and-forty-two, Tasman sailed the ocean blue. Good old Tas. *Zeelandia Nova*. One thin, ragged line on a snakes-and-ladder map, illuminated with winged, garlanded cherubs and Neptune seated on a chariot, drawn through the grey, stormy southern ocean by plunging nags, his nipple-titted Goddess by his side. He could do it under water, lucky bugger. Who knows where they are now—lying thigh on thigh beneath the icebergs that grind and grumble?

'Come on, Jacob. Now that we've come, what about a Corban's Dry?'
'Eh? Goodoh, Katus. Back in a jiff.' Off to the bar he plunges while the three-piece sinfonietta plays.

There they have the time of their life

'Hullo, Mr Small.'
'Hullo, Cheryl.'
Not bad. Miniskirt and suckity tits at full stretch. She must be catching her death of cold now that winter storm clouds gather. I should rub gums with this cherry-ripe before the trees lose all their leaves, and I lose all my strength.
'Tee hee. I'd like you to meet a friend of mine, Mr Small.'
Gorman stands disappearing into his beard. Her red fingers grip his frozen hand close to her pleated crotch.
'Pleased-to-meet-yer-I'm-sure.' Tee hee.
Gorman's eyes recede behind frenzied clouds of Players Navy Cut tobacco.
'Well, Cheryl, I may call you Cheryl, mayn't I? I must say I'm very pleased for the both of you. When's the big day?'
'Ooooooooooooooh, Mr Small.'
'Ha ha, I mustn't stand here keeping you apart. Good on yer both.' Back he goes. (Goodgod, if gimlet-eyed Gorman sees me dalling . . .)

'Look, Katus, this is bloody awful tonight. People from arsehole to breakfast time.'

'What are you crouching for?'
'Crouching? Um um. I've got one of me meegraines. Ooooohaaaaaah. I'm turribly sorry but I'll have to walk you to the bus and put you aboard. Do you mind? Oooooooohaaaaaah.'
And out they go. The yellow buses gather.
'Cheerio, Katus dalling, cheerio.'

Up the winding hill, Jacob slowly climbs, dreaming of the Tasman Sea, Katie's snuggle-tits and all the flowers that grow. An inky sky with great thundering balls of cloud, robins' nests and birds' trees, bending, binding and flying. He stops and looks high across the town, to the vast sprawling, humpy headland and the deep, sullen sea.

Now the southern sky is low, the shadows long, the rock is black and the sea lies darkly shining beneath the early evening moon. Seabirds are sleeping and washing themselves, plop-plopping into water cold, so cold the old rock aches where, on the encrusted stone embankment stands the steel gun, taken from the trench in France.
In this light the hills are black blood, and between the blue and scarlet buoys, the cold tide runs from the bay where *toi-toi* grows in grass once stained with seals' blood by the landing place, where the sealers worked and seagulls fed on crimson guts until they could no longer fly.

But now the grunting seal has gone, and empty is the cave where dusky plovers shiver in the weed that chokes this winter night. Amongst the lupins now, cold rain is falling from the south that blows a bitter wind across the dark peninsula. The headland cries and cliffs fall down, dying in the southern sea, breaking, turquoise turquoise, on the rock of waterfalls beautiful and streaming from the weed that heaves and clings to the blinded wave, fleeing north from dazzling walls of ice.

The fishing boat makes for home, and on the cliff the iceplant dies. Rain is in this cloud. Lost thistles blow away and down to the little bay of stone, where they drown in this night so black it drives the seabirds from their nests amongst roots of ancient trees, which this long night will fall and suck the bitter sap.
The bird will die,
the tree will fall,
and some time in the Spring,
driftwood on a northern beach
will float where pebbles shine
and children swim
and lovers lie
and this wind
never blows.

7

The traveller to Flagstaff by steamer finds himself, after he has passed the Heads, in the quiet waters of Macandrew Harbour, where a winding channel affords a water way to the City. The harbour is enclosed by low green hills once thickly covered with native bush, of which but scant vestiges remain. Passing Port Burns with its commodious docks and wharfs, the steamer follows a narrow strait between rocky islands whose summits are crowned with native shrubs and low trees, and even the steep faces afford a root-hold for bosky vegetation.

Root-hold? Root-hold? Bosky? Bosky?
'Hullo, Mr Small, I've come in to buy a book.'
Jacob looks up and sees her freshly scrubbed Monday-morning face. Every time I look at yooo, my heart goes boo boo boo. A root-hold in her bosky vegetation?
'Gooday, Cheryl, you're a sight for sore eyes. A book? So you had a few snorts with Mr Gorman on Friday night eh?'
'Aw, just a couple, tee hee.'
'How did you get to know him?'

'He buys his tobacco from our place.'
'Does he now? You want to be careful of him.'
'Why?'
'He's the Mad Doctor from Harley Street.'
'He's still a student.'
'Mad student then. Woe unto all them that come to know Gorman. Have you heard of Svengali?'
'No.'
'Well imagine a perverted Mandrake the Magician, Batman gone wrong, a turncoat Dr Kildare, a disease-ridden Ben Casey. That's Gorman.'
'What's he done?'
'What's he done?' Suck breath, dilate nostrils, grind teeth, roll eyes like jelly-beans, lean over counter to peer (undetected?) down her young, soft valley. 'Indescribable things, illegal operations, strange fiendish experiments on young girls. Aaaaaaaaagh.'
'Go on?'
'Hot gospel. Who knows what twisted paths the human mind may take? Who knows how deep is the bottomless pit of corruption?'
'Why hasn't he been executed or whatever they do to doctors?'
'Execrated. Why hasn't he been execrated? It is only I who knows the weird labyrinths of Gorman's frenzied mind. Since he was a child I've known. He comes to me for treatment, but his day of execration is not far off. What sort of a book do you want, love?'
'How can *you* treat him?'
'I read widely. Hubert Fink's *How to Overcome*

Nervous Tension, Sylvanus Stall's *What Every Young Man Should Know*. Bit of an expert reely. Ahem.'

'He's not very fast. That's all I can say. Not like somebody else I know, tee hee.'

'Do you want something spicy and riskay?' Uuuurgh.

'Ooooooh, yes. Something I can go to bed with.'

'You reckon I'm a bit faster than grisly Gorman, eh?'

'Well, you're not backward in coming forward.'

He looks at her ten-bob thrusters. 'Neither are you. Ha ha.'

She puts her plump hands on his counter. 'I never knock off till six.'

'*Forever Amber*. Have you read that?'

'No.'

He proffers the Digit paperback. 'Have a go on the house. A naughty on every page. Tremendous stuff. One of the great books in my life. When you've read it, we'll compare notes.'

'Goodoh, Jacob.' She grins and shrugs her bubs. 'I've got to go now, but I might see you tonight.'

'Rightoh.' Jacob stares after her across the counter. Ho hum, no rest (as they say) for the wicked.

Mr Aughatane emerges from the mysterious back like a withered oak on wheels, goes toward his pot of stew, stabs the cold contents with his woods of New Zealand ruler, shoves in the immersion heater and pulls the dangling cord. Underpants over tops of trousers, he stands, pulling at his hearing-aid flex and cleaning his ear with a Biro Retractable. He is joined by Mr

Doomsbury, bandy-legged and riding down the aisles of rare and wonderful books.
'Sheep four foot high they was.'
Shut up, Mr Doomsbury. The horse is dead. No sheep in this town. Ride to the kitchen for a bowl of soup. Join the Rechabites.

Aughatane inspects his culinary delight. 'I liked the look of your good lady, Mr Small. Heh heh.'
I bet you did, you dirty old bugger. Many's the bang you must have had on this very counter when this town was shining with gold, mined and sluiced from the mountain and the roaring river. Good lady? 'Ah, me sister, Mr A. Nice girl. I keep an eye on her now that father's passed away.' Sniff sniff. He buries his face into *Sunny Stories* and thinks of his Faraway Tree. Aughatane and Doomsbury crowd around the pot. Bubble bubble, toil and trouble, the stew is poured upon the plate. Gumbular mastication commences.
'There's a nail in me Irish.' Mr Doomsbury holds the slender instrument aloft before Aughatane's rheumy eye.
'A very nice young girl, Mr Small.'
'A nail, son, a nail. Something should be done. Awk awk.'
The wind blows under the door as the old men huddle. Aughatane goes through his Biblecards and Doomsbury's horny fingers shuffle *Best Bets*. (Ah, for foaming horses racing on northern sunny tracks, laughing girls in summer dresses.) Bless this shop. A

slater crawls across a thousand miles of art nouveau congoleum. The chairs creak. Someone has farted drumhead cabbage.
'Turrible. A nail. Turrible.'
Jacob holds his nose and consults his watch. Half past ten of a ninety-two hour day. 'Look, Mr A, I forgot to tell you that there's a sale of books on down at McPherson's. We might pick up a bargain or two. I'll be back in half an hour.' He makes for the door, breathing heavily through his respirator, and out into George Street he goes.

In this cold breathless wind, Jacob dreams of Paris in the Spring. Oh to be there when the government falls, to fight on the barricades; the roar of the Metro, direction Neuilly direction Vincennes; slender billowing girls floating on painted pleasure boats chuffing up the Seine. Je t'adore, voulez-vous caucher avec moi? Black coffee and rolls and a glass of absinthe at 5.30 a.m. Dodge the water-cart and laugh, chase the red balloon where the boy runs down shining cobbled streets. Sur le pont Clichy ici repose ma fille Dora. Toward the Octagon he strolls past Palmer's Pie Shoppe smelling of vats of ground beef and gallons of H.P. Sauce.

Flagstaff is singularly fortunate in the possession of many delightful walks in its immediate neighbourhood, the most verdantatious being the Octagon, a pretty little reserve with brilliant flower beds and rows of beautiful plane trees which line the road on either hand.

Dandle dandle down, the fairies fall on wrinkled heads nodding in the Octagon. Here the townsfolk sit, old legs apart fumbling with the button as the fairies fall. THE ALL POWERFUL GOD IS ALSO THE ALL LOVING GOD. The fairies fly and this wind blows. The traffic moves around the black Burns monument in this sun that chills an old man's bones, as they sit upon the slatted wooden seats in this cold and frosty morn, humming old songs to themselves. The stomachers are pulled from secret pockets, for soon it will be twelve o' clock and time for tea in the Kozee Cafe where they can sit and dream of golden days and girls upon their knees. IF YOU ARE LOOKING FOR A CHURCH HOME YOUR SEARCH HAS ENDED.

GOODmorning, Gladys. GOODmorning, Tom. GOODmorning, Claude. Coldsnap? Coff. Coff. Coldsnap?

She lost her last you know, a cryingshame, but I expect they'll try for another.

Black in the basket, the Flagstaff mothers trundle, proud to boot for job-lots of china birds, skeins of wool, hand-woven balaclavas and vyella underpants. Look-at-the-daisies-Daph. Such-a-nice-show.

Around they go, sniffing at the bargains, waddling arm in arm, string bags full of sausages and pounds of porridge for the gut. Up his fundamental orifice, the old men mouth encrusted jokes and fiddle with their

bums as this winter comes, creeping into parking
lots, where once proud turrets stood before the wood
had rotted in the beam that grew a hundred years
upon the hill.
Howareya, Kinney? The walkingstick is still and stiff
between their thighs as they rub their tweedy knees.
Heh heh. The blood is black and cold upon the chin.
And Robbie Burns sits proud, his back against the
hill.

'Gooday, Jacob. What are you doing out this time of
day?'
Ka-ka-ka-Katie, Ka-ka-ka-Katie, you're the one that I
adore. Beating hearts and pounding steam trains it
is she. 'Gooday, Kate (leather flat-heeled shoes, denim
shirt, black hair to be lost in forever, and breasts like
mounds of warm-cut hay) I've just been to McPherson's to get a barg or two. (She is gentle-eyed and Irish
beautiful.) They've got a real list today: menus from
the Glasgow Pie Palace, prospectuses from Hyatt's
Turkish Turkish, Russian Sulphur and Vapour
Baths, programmes from the Princess Theatre, gas-lit,
lofty and well ventilated, a good supply of water with
firehoses and buckets always in readiness, burnt down
with six lives lost in 1904. Hee haw. What about a
sandwich and a nice hot cup of tea?'
'Okay, dal. What about the old Savoy?'
Hand in hand, they walk across the frosty grass,
through golden poplar trees, and all is dance and
breathless for a time as blow leaves blow around the
Octagon, so gold they fly and flutter through the

stippled sky to fall on old men's heads. The poplars are the first to turn, then the oak that soon will droop its scaly arms and sleep a long, cold season.

GENTS' CLOAKS LADIES' POWDER ROOM, antedeluvian droppings in the brass tureen that stands on massive old mahogany. Tudor style, hot-house flowers bloom in marble vases by walls of panelled oak. Through the door they go. The plate glass is stained with steam and fingerprints as Jacob cogitates upon a place to sit. Hand in hand, they go down the aisle between the dark and grainy tables, row on row in this vast dining hall. Tasselled chandeliers gleam in varnished gloom where wall plaques hang by faded Elizabethan galleons on waves of scaly blue. By leadlight windows the dusty velvet hangs. Jacob stares around this high-class lounge, where Flagstaff's maiden ladies sit in suits of Scottish tweed and English leather brogues.

'Ah, Katus, you, me and the old Savoy, Flagstaff's coffee palace of yester-year. Look, here's a nice spot. Full view of all proceedings.'
'What proceedings?'
'Aw, you never know in this place. You know it's a front for a luxuriously appointed brothel?'
'Haw.'
'No-kid. Many's the time I've seen the mayor coming out from between those Japanese dragon pisspots doing up his fly. It's really weird out the back: fur chains, newspaper jockstraps, wind-up mechanical

dildos, vats of duggity-doo paint, the lot. Many's the time I've revealed it all to the editor of the *Flagstaff Daily Times*, but the bugger's never had a bar of it. The paper probably runs the place. I'll drop in and see the Moderator next week.'

'Dildos? Duggity-doo paint?'

A girl with two-inch breasts in smock appears. Tea and cakes for two?

'Gooday, Min. I've developed a bit of an allergy to butterfly cakes this season.'

But she has gone through the swinging doors.

'What did you get at McPherson's, Jacob?'

'Eh? Aw, one or two bargains. A photo of an 1889 Marshall 4 h.p. portable steam thrashing machine, two gilt-bound ledgers from the Dickens Fellowship, the 1928 minutes from the Soroptimists Club, a clamshell from the Great Barrier Reef . . .'

'I thought old Aughie was only in books.'

'Crickeydick, you're right. Nevermind, I'll take it home to son Gideon.'

'Son Gideon?'

'Uuuuuuuuuurrrgh (heaving cream cakes and dreadful heart palpitations) me sister Brenda's kid, just like me own son reely, dreadful case, turrible-turrible, she got done over by three fellers when she was gathering rock specimens on the railway track down at Palmerston. She's a dedicated amateur rock-hunter, specialising in railway stones. A brilliant career ruined. Tsk tsk.'

'Jacob, I thought your sister's name was Jacqueline.'

'There's two: Brenda and Jacqueline, they've both

got sons, Gideon and Dennis, one's widowed and one's divorced . . .'
'And they've both been raped?'
'Yeh. Turrible double tragedy. You wouldn't read about it. It never rains but it pours. Many hands make light work. Grief has really come to our family, what with Mum and Dad coughing it and all, and me left to carry the burden, there's little enough I get out of life I always say.'
'I never know when to believe you, Jacob. You're always off somewhere, why don't you move in with me?'
'Move in with you? Katus pet, nothing would give me greater pleasure (and I mean it) but there's Jacqueline and Brenda and Gideon and Dennis and the chooks and the farm and the horse.'
'Have you got a horse too?'
'Yup. A big red gelding. Mighty beast left to us by Uncle Albert, eats a bale of hay.'
'How do you manage on what you get from the shop?'
'Bit of a struggle (pulls his long, droughty, *Grapes of Wrath* face) but we get there. Sell eggs, the two girls take in tatting, in fact there could be a fortune in tatting, a bloody fortune, if you really organised the outworkers, Flagstaff women love tatted tablecloths, doileys, earmuffs, the lot, and Mrs Dolan nextdoor helps out. Look Katus, what's happened to Minnie Mouse? I could eat a horse (Uuuuuurk) Ah (thankgod) here she is. Gooday, Min, has the Lord Mayor been in lately?' But she has come and gone, her white high heeled shoes rattling like rodents' bones on the

parquet floor. 'Nice girl that. A bit on the thin silent side, she comes into the shop now and then for weight-increasing books. Have a sandwich, love. Marmite and Lettuce? Fishpaste and Lettuce? Bakedbean and Lettuce? Marmite and Cucumber?'
Katie looks at him. 'Well, dalling, if we go on, I'll have to meet your sisters sooner or later. They might not like me.'
'Try the fishpaste, Katie. Yum yum.'
'What's your address?'
'Where?'
'At Woodstock?'
'What's Woodstock?'
'Where you live, silly.'
'Aw, Woodstock, um um, Bannockburn Road, you'd never find it, even I get foxed, bloody maze of unmade roads, dirt tracks, farmlets, piggeries, barns, sheds, why Uncle Albert ever lived there I'll never know. Try the cucumber: non-fart producing variety, I can always tell.'
'Well, one of these nights, I'll come up with you to see the children.'
'Christus-a-um, look Kate, there's the Lord Mayor going through the bat-wings. Bloody old McKechnie having his bit of fun. That's where it is—out the back of the kitchen. I bet they've pressed poor old Min into service. Disgusting.' He wipes his mouth. 'Not bad sangers at all. I must get the recipe from Min when next we have a picknose up at the Groynes.' He takes her cool hand. 'Well, pet, I must be off to McPherson's, they've got a sale on.'

'I thought you'd just come from McPherson's?'
'Eh? That's right. I've got to go back and have a look at their incunablua. I think I saw two 1926 ledgers of the Belleknowes Pipe Band Society. Worth a fortune.'
'Will you be coming around tonight?'
'Wild horses couldn't keep me away, Katus. I'll bring a bottle of Corban's and we'll toast muffins on the fire. When Irish eyes are smiiiiiiiiling, dum diddy dum. Men must work while women weep. (Jug jug) Golly Moses, Kat, golly Moses.'
He supposes.

8

Half past six and all is dark.
KAAAAAAPOOOOOOW. Bucks a black V8, James Deaned from deserts of vast eternity. The YMCA neon glitters: ANYONE CAN HATE IT COSTS TO LOVE. Buses groan, the corner lavatory squirts and sighs. The street is empty but for this old car heaving in the dark. Television and tea. All our Lord's children are snug-me-downed in their beds, tucked in their blankets like little Nanook of the North in his kayak canoe. Ten thousand fires are red and clinkering in the grate. Jacob crosses the street as the traffic lights stare, their steel circuits clicking like robots from the vast, outer space. The lights are still on in McDee's Saloon, and in the window he peers at pyramids of Brylcream and Palmolive Soap. Gillette Blue Blades and Vaseline Hair Tonic, Capstan Plain, a lone Peterson pipe balanced on piles of Bears Dark and king-size display packs manufactured in the wide, warm, temperate Marlboro Country. Where is my cheery little bird, Cheryl, this dark and vacant night? Being shagged by some muscled, heavy-tooled lad,

sired from sprawling slopes of scree and shifting black moraine.

Suddenly the lights go out and the door opens.
'Hullo, Mr Small. Is that you?'
The old heart sinks and rises. He peers toward the door.
'Ha ha. Didn't think you'd be here so late tonight.'
She does her grin. 'I'm just locking up. Mr McDee's down with the flu today. Is there anything I can do?'
'Ah there's a lot of it about with this cold weather and all.'
He smells her June Roses Toilet Soap and considers. 'You couldn't get me a packet of Pall Mall Filter, could you?'
'Never too late for a customer like you, Mr Small, tee hee.'
She opens the door and steps back inside. 'Come on, I'll see what I can find.'
His whole world is waiting, he consults his watch and follows her into the shop.
I'll just pull down the blind if you don't mind. Can't get caught after hours.' She leans across great geometries of splitting cardboard boxes and pulls the slender cord, (legs and leather boots, skirt rises, suspenders embedded in her thighs, are those her floral pants he can see?) then disappears beyond to the barber's shop. One fifteen-candle-power lamp gleams.

Hair-Gro, Esquire Deodorant, Souvenir Flagstaff spoons, the barbers' chairs stand bolted to the floor.

draped in patched sheets like old men sleeping, knees raised heavenward toward the painted Victorian ceiling. An old, bald broom, vague traces of hair, baskets of greasy tissue, the smell of bay-rum, a lone tap drips, piles of *Pix* and *Australasian Post*, WE SEND TO HOBART. Balkan Sobranie from across the sea. (Where is Hobart? Where is across the sea?) Yellow, speckled mirrors with Chesterfield stickers. KING SIZE SATISFIES.

'Come on down the back,' she calls, 'come and see my stock.' Her stock? Hum hum. He parts the dull green curtain to find her standing there proffering the merchandise, the red packet held in her thick, jolly hands.

'Here you-are, Mr Small. I found it first time round.' In the gloom her index finger tickles his outstretched palm. 'Have this on the house.'

'Aw, I couldn't really. Let me pay for it.'

She comes up close and her strong, white teeth shine. 'Nah, come on Jacob, you're a regular customer. Old man McDee won't miss it.'

He feels her fingernails as he takes the packet. Great balls of meat, she is close as she breathes with her breasts stuffed with milk and muscle. Spring heifers, strong, young bobby calves struggling in bales, she takes his arm and shows him everything she's got.

'Old McDee's worth thousands. I've just been stock-taking, so I know.'

'I wouldn't like to take this stock, ha ha.'

'I bet you would with me.'

'Well, with you . . .'

She nudges him with her hip and removes her turquoise knit.
'*Forever Amber*'s a real dag.'
'Thought you'd like it.'
'You've watched me around town a lot, haven't yoo?'
'Well (ahem) you're a *very* attractive girl.'
'And that's why you always buy your ciggies here?'
Ciggies. Uuuuurk. Deep breath. 'Ah, you're a fine sight to a young working man first thing in the morning.' A fine sight indeed with all that meat and no potato.
She fronts up close, grinning and touching him with her body.
'What do you think of my figure?'
'Your figure? Ah, very alooring, very well developed.'
He touches the left one with his finger.
'Ooooh, you shouldn't do that.'
'Very tasty, very sweet.'
'Ooooh.'
She is rolling like a ship at sea as he tweaks her mammaries.
'Ooooh.'
She grabs both his hands and keeps them there, hee hee, puts her lips on his and fills his mouth with her strong pink tongue as they grip, she using her thigh to part his legs in this dark of multi-coloured showcards, day-glo signs and cartons of freshly packed tobacco. Cheryl yum yum, he lifts her skirt and runs his finger around her stocking tops, suspender buttons, her belt and bum, she wriggles, shows her tongue and shoves

her hand inside his strides, stands on one leg, removes a boot, then the other.

'Just a tick, I'll have to get me sussies off.'

Sussies?

'Come on, Jacob, we can do it on the chair outside.' She stuffs her pants into a boot. 'Come on, take yours off, easy as pie.'

Oooooooh, he cups her mount with his hand and fiddles her with his finger, she pulls him by his handle. Click, out go the lights in McDee's Saloon, old floorboards creak as she pulls him across the worn congoleum, her skirt is raised above her waist and her bare bums gleam.

'Ooh, Jacob, you're a dag.'

His great masthead up, she sits him on the throne, then she mounts him, arms about his body sighing like a train, she bends straight back cables on the creak, she is over him, rise her mountains high on high, she sucks him up clambering country girl in draughty barns of hay, the wind blows beneath the door, she is strong and built for bairns as he screws her up, thick in the muscle, she rides like a hunter, stomach, buttock and thigh, giggles tickles and sighs for the stormy strength of the ruck and fuck of this draughty mirrored world. Up and down she rides to beat the band and takes him stiff and sheer up the rocky chasm where he can neither see nor hear nor breathe and now suck sucks him in silver spurts like froth upon the mountain stream that flows, so cold, so cold, so cold.

'Jacob Small,' she sighs, 'you're a real dag.'

'And by Christus, Cheryl me love, you're a real dag too.'

Filled to the brim, he goes home through winding labyrinths of rusted iron and hanging stone.

9

At Jacob's house high upon the hill, the evening trees grow and the kitchen fire burns while Gorman sips his sherry and schemes as Jacquie, brown bottle in hand, looks at him and considers.

['When he comes to know the state of her feelings toward him, he should pretend to be ill . . . he should intentionally hold her hand and place it on his eyes and forehead, and under the pretence of preparing some medicine for him, he should ask her to do the work for his own sake in the following words.']
'This work should be done by you and nobody else.'
'What work, Gorman?'
'Jacqueline, my dear, I haven't told you this before, but I haven't been feeling the best for some time.'
Puff puff.
'What's up?'
'I have in fact been treating myself so far, but I think I'll have to ask for another opinion.'
She sits on the couch beside him, her hair freshly washed, smelling of skin perfume, white cardigan, black bra underneath, skirt well above her knees.

'Poor Gorman.'

He levers his cherrywood from his teeth and searches for his multi-purpose-prodder-tamper. 'Up to date, I've been on N-Acetyl-p-aminophenol, but I'm afraid to say it hasn't done me much good.' He fumbles in his pocket and withdraws a bottle of coloured pills. 'I wonder if you would be so good as to get me a glass of water and administer me these tablets.'

She looks at him, gets up and goes to the kitchen as he watches her slender buttoned back. ['This device of illness should be continued for some three days and three nights.'] Through the kitchen door he sees her stretch for a glass, her cardigan lifting to show her white belly. The tap runs.

'You don't want me to give them to you, do you?'

'Well, I feel so bloody awful. I was wondering if you would.'

She returns and sits beside him once more, turns (skirt riding up again) and puts the glass to his lips. 'Now where are the pills?'

(My God it's working.) He places two in her hand and feels the moist, cool palm.

'Come on, Gorman, you can't be that bad. Surely you can take them yourself.'

He swallows them down (quick-glances at her breasts) and stretches out his body, closing his eyes and sighing.

'Well, you're neither use to man nor beast, are you? How long is this going to go on?'

'My prognosis is for three days and three nights.'

'Good Lord, it's only the flu. You *are* an old hypo.'

'I'm not a hypo, Jacqueline, not at all. It's some kind of virus.'

'Well,' she sighs, 'you aren't much good to me lying around the place.'

'Not much good to you?'

'I like my men to be healthy and not dying everywhere.'

'You haven't got any men, Jacqueline. Have you?'

'Oh, I've had three or four.'

'But not since you've been married?'

'Not since I've been married, but there's a first time for everything, isn't there, Gorman?'

He peers through his eyebrows, shifts his pipe and places his hand upon her knee. She looks at him, bulky, bearded and breathing heavily. 'How's your head now?'

'It's going. Pseudo Hydrochloride was always very good.'

'I'm glad to hear that. Would you like a sherry?'

Gorman runs his forefinger around his collar and looks at his under-water Oyster Rolex chronometer. Six o' clock. 'What time will Jacob be in?'

'Between eight or nine. He's never home before that.' She leans across to the table and gets the bottle. (Her back this time and a trace of her little pink half-slip.) 'I think he's carrying on.' Sniff sniff.

'I wouldn't say that, Jacqueline.'

'Well, I would. For what other reason would he be out all the time?'

Gorman starts probing, tamping and igniting, his big

hands gripping the Algerian briar bowl. 'As far as I know, Jacqueline, he's got the shop and Mr Aughatane can't be up to much these days.'

'Up to much? The story I get is that the old man's a terrible slave-driver. Works the whole night through, moving stock, taking stock, selling stock, but where the customers come from, God only knows.'

Pope Gorman the Pius: 'I must say that there's never anyone there when I go in.'

'Exactly. What does he do all day—and half the night? I wish I'd never come to this beastly town. Bloody cold wind day after day, no entertainment, never get out of this flat, no one to talk to, and the way Jacob's going, or not going, we'll be here all our bloody lives.'

Dr Gorman, Superintendent of City Hospital: 'Well, when I graduate, Flagstaff's not going to be much use to me.' She takes his glass and fills it again.

'When *do* you graduate, Gorman?'

'Next year, Jacqueline, next year. I've done very well you know, even if I say it myself. And after that (broad chest swelling) it's the big city lights and a lucrative practice for me.'

'How nice for you Gorman. And I'll still be stuck here.' She pulls a Kleenex from the top of her skirt and applies it to a moist blue eye.

'Now come on, Jacqueline, I'm sure that won't happen. Jacob only needs a bit of direction and pushing from a good woman like you.'

'I don't feel like being a good woman any more. I'm sick of being a good woman.'

Gorman slides his hand over her patella. 'Any time, Jacqueline, you know you can come to me.'

She takes another sherry, stretches some more and lets her head fall upon his shoulder. 'Let's change the subject. What have you been reading lately?'

He puts down his pipe, transfers his glass and slides his arm along the top of her sofa. 'You might be surprised to know, the *Kama Sutra* (he pauses for effect) it does have quite a medical interest, certainly an historical one.'

She looks at him through her empty glass. 'Tell me about it, Gorman, tell me.'

Gorman lowers his arm from the top of the sofa, cranes a look at the Rolex, swills his sherry like a mouthwash and decides to take the plunge. 'Well, Jacqueline dear, um ah, there are three kinds of kiss . . .'

'And what are they?'

Her cashmere knit is soft beneath his hand, and under that, her shoulder. 'The, ah, nominal kiss, the touching kiss, and the, ah, throbbing kiss.'

'What about showing me the throbbing kiss?'

Underneath the white wool, her bra is black and beautiful.

'Look, Jacqueline dear, you've always known how I've . . . but you're a married woman.'

'Not only am I a married woman, Gorman, but I've also decided to enjoy myself and become modern. It's little enough *I* get out of life.' She hiccups, turns close to Gorman's Harris tweed, puts her hands inside and whispers in his ear. 'You want to (fuck) me don't you?'

'F**k you? How much sherry have you been having this afternoon?'

She opens her lips and takes another tot. 'I've always wanted to be (fucked) by a man who wears a beard.'

'F****d by a man who wears a beard?'

She runs her hands under his pits, puts her sherry mouth on his and bites his lower lip, another hiccup, then sighs, 'Do you love me, Gorman?'

'Ja-jacqueline, I've always loved you.'

'Love me now then.'

'Now?'

'There's no time like the present, is there?'

'What if Jacob comes in?'

'He won't.'

'But what if he does?'

'Look, Gorman *darling*, for the last two years Jacob's not been home before eight o'clock at the earliest, why should he change tonight? Why did you come around this afternoon anyway?'

Gorman sucks at his mustache and moistens his mouth. 'Well, ah um ah, after what you said last Saturday I thought I'd drop by if I was passing.'

'Look, darling, you've had your hand on my knee for the last fifteen minutes. It's either got to go up or go down.'

'Ah ah (pant pant, heave heave) Jacqueline *sweet*heart . . .' He knocks off another Corban's Dry and starts the uncertain exploration of her Ivory Coast. Valentino Gorman, the Great Lover: 'Jacqueline, Jacqueline, you have the most beautiful body (surgeon's scalpel up to the rim of her pants) purrfectly formed ah ah.'

'Have I, Gorman dear?' She grabs his beard and kisses him, her snakey little tongue ferreting in his mouth. 'Let's (wriggle wriggle) get off this uncomfortable sofa (probe probe) and get on the bed.'

'But what if (self-administered oral resuscitation), what if Jacob comes home?'

'Gorman (wriggle out of cashmere, hands behind back undoing buttons *seriatim*, pointing her perties straight at him) I thought medical students were the randiest of them all. You don't seem to qualify.'

'Randy? Randy? Of course I'm randy. I've loved you right from the start . . .'

'Love me now then.'

Cut to the bearded quick, he leaps, great groping hugs and hairy kisses, hands tapping the knobs of her slender spine, he lurches after her as she escapes to the master bedroom. Click goes the light, a hundred frenzied puff-puffs, carpenter thumbs pulling at belt and buttons, Harris tweed sportscoat (with leather arm-patches), striped winter shirt, tweed trousers (with buttoned fly), underpants, number 11 toe-capped brogues, woollen socks, hornrimmed glasses (for astigmatism) and lumbrous leaps into bed.

'Mmmmmmm, Gorman, you *are* (hiccup) a lovely big man . . .'

The warm sheets rise and fall, noses knock and knees collide as they fly blind through the early night. Outside, the old tree whispers as Jacquie utters a

triumphant sound. Gorman shakes and thinks, my God is that the sound Phut? Phat? Sut? or Plat?
Thus starts the union of the bull and the deer.

Jacob comes through his front gate. Ho hum, *Chez Miffawney* and *Chez Small*. A great place this mansion where we all live, nicely situated in the teeth of the southerlies. Leaf mould on Mrs Miffawney's washing from the trees that spread their roots and crack the old crazy-paving. Black birds and convolvulus, creeper climbing on the creaking garage, and cloud upon the hill. The seeds of grass choke the drains, the bush is coming close and strong, dark roots twist and split the walls of empty cellars. Mrs Miffawney's old car squats on wooden blocks, stiff in the back, spiders in the steering wheel, birds' nests in the canvas hood, the rumble seat is empty. By the path a gnome lies dying, its little blue concrete jacket crumbling and hidden in fennel and silver weed, the yellow green shoots growing over plywood chests imported long, long ago from China and Ceylon. Old iron gates and pillars of stone, the shingle piles high and moss grows up the crack. The scythe is snapped. The bird will soon have this place for its own and feed on the bulbous marrows running wild and twisting through the fence. And in the dark evening, nature's creatures will come to stake their claim: the opossum with its shining eye, the bellbird, the kingfisher, the silver eye, morepork and the laughing owl. With the wind and the hill they come, and bring their young to this garden and the empty house, creaking, sighing, dying.

Mrs Dolan is in her garden, hacking at the frost, carting frozen fowlshit to the hole to prepare it for the Spring. Jacob watches her bending by the light of her hurricane lamp; peastakes quiver as she thrusts them deep into the earth. 'Gooday, Mrs Dolan. How's the old night shift going?'
'A great day, Mr Small.'
In the light of her lamp she holds a dead willow shoot aloft. 'Compost, compost. Good for me asparrowgrass.'
'I thought early Spring was best for asparrowgrass.'
'So it is, so it is, but the sooner me pit's prepared the better.'
'One of these days, Mrs D, I wouldn't mind having a look at your pit.'
'Any time, Mr Small, any time.'
Jacob walks through the wicker gate and decides to see how his bantams are doing before going in to tea.

The southern moon is up as he takes the winding gravel path through the sodden, misty garden to the house where his feathered friends live.
'Chooook chook-chook-chook.'
Pigeons bawbling in the empty birdbath, the smell of last summer's cabbages in the broken glasshouse. Cling cling, a skylark swoops, sings and sweeps into the valley below. The wind blows and the night-world trembles.
'Mr Small?' Florence Nightingale of the Garden

returns with her guttering lamp. Dig, hack, sow, mulch, fertilise and grow. Personalised night-soil in kiddies' plastic buckets. In the lamplight, Jacob sees her leaning on her rake, powdering a sheeps' turd expertly between her forefinger and thumb. Mrs Dolan snaps a tulip bulb with her other thumb and stands in her nightflying boots breaking ice as she fills her wooden cart. Handmade sox, old musquash coat and clear plastic-mac, a tea-towel covers her Toni perm, and over that a rain hat of polythene in case the heavens leak. 'Going to feed your chooks?'

'Aye, Mrs D, aye.' Jacob strikes a match and ferrets in the woodshed for his bag of mash, finds and lights a candle, tosses aside an old cane, a priceless jardiniere, gilt picture frame, bits of wormy timber from warm, moist, northern forests. Aha, a number 2 wood with insulation tape handle. He goes outside for a few practice swings. It is I, Dr Carey Middlecoff. A birdie 3 on the second dog's leg hole.

'I reckon they've gone clucky, Mr Small.'

'Not correct, Mrs D. I've got four dozen in the last few days. Me Loved Ones are all egg-bound. Mighty layers. My ladywife's going to enter the Preserved Egg Section of the Royal Flagstaff Winter Show.'

'They look clucky to me.'

'Eggs everywhere. If I wasn't so kind-hearted I could make a fortune from these banties.' The mash is tossed, cluck, cluck, cluck.

'You shouldn't have chooks in a built-up area.'

'Get clucked.'

'Lowers the tone of the street.'

There's a long, long trail a-winding, ba ba ba ba ba, boo boo.
'I wonder Mrs Miffawney allows it.'
Chooooook, chooooook, chooooook.
'What do you do with the manure?'
'Make it into snuff. There's nothing like a miniscule of fowlturd up your left snoz, it cleans up the old sinuses and antrems, releases the flow of your vital nasal juices, which, when they flow at the rate of two pints a day, ensure health and regularity.'
'Eh?'
'I can't marry you, Mrs Dolan, but we'll always be good friends.'
'If you've got any to spare, I'll use it on me triambles.'
'Triambles? Hey, Mrs D, your moles are falling off. I'll hop inside and get a paper bag.' He picks up the golf-stick and disappears. On to the landing and up the stairs and through the door. 'Hey, Jackers, sorry I'm late, trouble on the estate, cluckiness everywhere. Mrs Dolan's arse is enough to put any bird off laying. Jacquie?' He looks. 'Aaah, gooday, Gorman, gooday.'

'Gorman, I'd like you to meet my principal (ahem) Mr Thos McD. Aughatane and his life-long friend [and partner in crime] Mr Alfred Doomsbury.'
The veiny hands are shaken.
'Sheep four feet high they was.'
Jacob bends to Gorman's ear. 'Old Doomo's got a chronic case of sheeping sickness, he used to shag the young ones in the high country when he was a lusty young lad sixty year ago. I'll be loving *ewe* always, ha hem haw. A stout and raspberry for Mr Aughatane, sir, and a portergaff for Mr D? Hey, Claudine, hey hey?'
Aughatane and Doomsbury hunch eagle-like over the bar and watch as the demon alcohol is poured. The Munster Arms, Flagstaff's finest hostelry, also designed by Mr Boldini and built in 1892. Solid mahogany bars four feet wide, ceramic pumps with blue and white William Morris decorations, gothic stained glass, hand-painted murals: *The Story of Flagstaff*, gold-framed masterpieces: *The Founding of the Bank of England A.D. 1694, The Head of Lake Grynant N. Wales, The Last Piece of Bread*, the

Voltaic dredging gold from the river Clutha in the year of our Lord, 1900. (Aughatane is served and sucks his stout and raspberry.) Then, the sounds of stamps and poppet-heads echoed down the gorge where the hydraulic sluices tore the shingle from the golden river, as the dredges smoked and steamed and thrashed with chains and buckets brimmingful with ore floated fifteen score of companies. The Stock Exchange was overflowing then with copperplate ledgers, sharebrokers and investors, the stakes were high as bowler-hatted business men gambled at the gleaming tables. Monte Carlo, Faro, Euchre, all the games were played recklessly by the bearded patriarchs who owned great consortiums. *Electric, Voltaic, Magnetic, Lady Ranfurly*, the dredges stripped and sluiced the river of its gold three thousand days and nights while the hawk and the mountain parrot watched, perched high upon the peaks.

The barmaid pushes at her cuticles and picks her nose beneath a framed water-colour of *H.M.N.Z.S. Achilles at the River Plate 1940*, two draped cut-out flags and an All Blacks' Calendar. She applies Cutex to her fingernails, sits on a case of empties and plucks at her eyebrows with a hammer thumb. Jacob lifts the perspex cover from the complimentary counter-lunch and fills his mouth with Bycrofts Crackers and N.Z. Cheddar cheese. 'Good to see you, Gorman. You're a a real Briton, as they say, looking after Jackers in me hour of business need. Christ, I've been busy these past few weeks, the two financial gentlemen over there have really kept me on my toes. A friend in need is a friend indeed, ha ha.' Gorman's thick fingers twitch open a fresh packet of Hollandia Aromatic and the tender, choice leaf is teased, rubbed and ground. Jacob crooks his wrist and takes another cracker. 'However, the financial crisis should soon be over and I'll be back with me loved-ones at the hearth and home.'

'Well it has occurred to me sometimes, Jacob, that Jacqueline must be short of company now and then, and I am not obliged to keep regular business hours.'

'Short of company? By Jove, yes. Frankly, Gorman, I'm playing for very high stakes at the present time. It's not all pressing the tit on the old cash register and selling Ethel M. Dell y'know. Overdrafts, cash flows, liquidity, debentures, interest rates, insecured mortgages, P & L Accounts, stock re-de-valuation, loans on third recall at seven and three quarters per cent compound interest falling due at the first of the month, trial balance sheets and budget allocations on open-to-close and open-to-buy. I've lost a bit of weight this last month through worry watching the old share columns in the F.D.T.'s indices, by Jove, by Jove.'

Gorman grips his pipe. 'F.D.T.'s indices?'

'But it's a great life if you don't weaken. Jacquie and I are very fond of you. What about shouting my financial colleagues a drink?'

Gorman digs into his pigskin wallet and a further round of drinks is bought.

'If you want to be in on some very important deals,

Gorman, you might also buy me and me colleagues some lunch.'

'Well um ah, I do have to be back at Pathology by two.'

'Dr Gorman, gentlemen, has generously offered to treat us to lunch.'

Aughatane and Doomsbury put their glasses down on the mahogany counter, adjust their bifocals and stare at the Munster Arms menu. Heh heh, pre-historic glands start to pump overtime at the thought of this toothsome provender.

'You won't regret this little generosity, Gorman. Holy Moses, Aughie and Dooms run this town financially. Don't let appearances fool you. Many's the time I've seen them wheeling and dealing over the tables at the Flagstaff Club. It's old Aughie who supplies the real info to the Financial Editor of the F.D.T. I'm planning to retire in a year or so, ahem.'

'Look, Jacob, I really don't think . . .'

No. 1. BRAIZED SAUSAGES WITH MASHED POTATO AND PEAS.

The gastric juices flow.

'Gorman, didn't I see you down at the Tasman with that girl from McDee's the other night?'

No. 4. PIE PEAS AND SAUCE.

Orgasmic pissings in the mouth.

The big doctor flushes, takes off his glasses and squints.

'I can still see you, Gorman, ha-ha, I can still see you.'

'I get my pipe tobacco there (puff puff) and I just

happened (fiddle fiddle) to knock into her at the (tamp tamp) bar.'
No. 5. TOMATO AND SAUSAGES ON TOAST.
The juices rush through crusty tubes.
'You want to watch that girl, Gorms, I know how you meds go round dipping your wicks in southern quarters, and as a married business man . . .'
'Look, Jacob, I really don't think . . .'
'Unimpeachable sources have informed me that that girl (whatshername?) has been prodded like a pincushion since she left Flagstaff Girls' High School . . .'
No. 7. POACHED EGG AND PEAS ON TOAST.
Pancreatic eruptions and surgings in choked canals.
'. . . stuffed like a bolster, rooted like a rata stump, if you'll excuse the patois.' He leans over seniorstatesmanlike and talks in Gorman's ear. 'She's carrying the old dreaded D., you know.'
'Jacob, you-don't-think . . .'
'Well, gentlemen, what's it to be? We'll have another round per favour Dr Gorman, Claudine, if you don't mind.'
The girl sets down her Cutex sachet and moves toward the bottles.

Jacob tackles his Savory Mince on Toast. 'Many thanks ta ye, Gormo, this is just the thing to get me going through a hard financial afternoon, a most victacular spread to keep the liver free from all impurities. I'll mention your name kindly when the empire is split up.'
'Jacob, I must get down to Pathology.'

'Your blood's worth bottling, Gorman.'
Gorman moves toward the door. 'I'll see you later then.'
'Call at the house any time. Wipe your feet on the welcome mat, you're a real white man.'
'Cheerio, then.'
'You're straight out of the box, a number one candidate, one of nature's gentlemen.'
Gorman's big, tweedy body is jammed between the double sand-blasted doors.
Haw haw.

Aughatane and Doomsbury dredge their sunken canals and suck their bony gums. Ho hum, Jacob stares out the window at the day. Half-past-one, still cold, and starting to rain. He thinks of roast potatoes, slices of hot roast beef and rich brown gravy; of mulled wine and baked granny-smith apples with clotted cream and cloves. Sudden joy, it is Katie's half day off.
'Look, Mr Aughatane, sir, McPherson's have a complete set of fifty-eighth reprint Edgar Rice Burroughs. Priceless, priceless? Me buy? Me buy? (Chung-king-chong-ah-so, a million Charlie Chan bows and thrice million kow tows, Harry Houdini's famous disappearing act when tied with chains inside a bucket of water) ahem, goodbye, Mr Aughatane, goodbye.'

'Jacob, what are you doing here this time of day?'
'Aw, bit pissed off.' He looks at her and goes in to smells of Johnson's Baby Powder, fresh unironed

washing, raw vegetables in wicker baskets, piles of old fashion magazines from the Library, and Katie.
'Old Augh thinks I'm at McPherson's again. But I thought I'd come to see yooo-hooo-hooo-hooo-hooo-hooo-hooo. Slim Whitman's a great yodeller, don't you think?'
'Jacob love, you might lose your job.'
'Nah, Katus, Aughie never knows whether he's on his arse or his elbow. How's things down at the bones factory?'
'Um, lugged a few bodies this morning. Cockies with bad backs keep me going. It's the provincial fogs, Jersey cows and early morning milking sheds, up to their knees in milk and water they are, most of the time. Want a fag, dalling?'
'I wouldn't say no, Katie, I wouldn't say no.'
'And a drop of dry?'
'Yum yum.'
She comes up close and gives him the glass, and he peers down her denim shirt. 'Why do you wear those bloody awful singlets, Kate?'
'They're not singlets, they're men's T-shirts.'
'Why do you wear them then?'
'They keep the cold out of me kidneys.'
Through the window, Jacob sees the purplegrey clouds lumbering over the crenellated turrets of Flanagan's Brewery, and across the bay runs the sea, runs the sea south from the Golden Gate to the castle crumbling on the headland; in the unknown hinterland the frost is glistening in southern scree sprawling slopes of sheer, where deep are the miners' graves in

caverns vast of ice, the wheel is split, the fruit has ripened, the fence has fallen, now drifts the smoke north from rocks of winter.

'Jacob?' Katie has put a record on her player (she really is nice, mussed up dark hair, breasts comfortable, ha ha, one of her stockings is wrinkled, Irish eyes and freckles all down her arms). 'Hey, bet you can't guess who this is.'
Music plays from the old HMV, thirties number, familiar trumpet, doo wah wah wah.
'Ummmmmm, that's the Dorsey Brothers.'
'Yeh, but who's the vocalist?'
Listen listen listen. 'Oh Christ I give up, who's the vocalist?'
She sucks a hairpin and unpins her wrinkled stocking. 'Jo Stafford.'
'Shit. Forgotten all about her. How much is that dogeeee in the window, the one with the waggly taaaaaaail?'
She throws her nylons on the sofa, gets up and moves around the house, picks up her Japanese guitar and plays one chord as the Dorsey Brothers blow, turns a page on the Saints' Calendar, winds her Westclox and disappears into the kitchen. Bras and cotton-tail pants on the clothes horse. Readers' Digest Book Club Books, a packet of Paton & Baldwins knitting needles, an empty bottle of Chanel No. 5, Whitman's *Leaves of Grass*. 'Oh Jesus,' from the kitchen she grumbles, 'I've got no fucking coffee.'
'Why don't you ever use lipstick, Katus?'

'Like me lips naked.'

The record player has stopped and hums as Jacob sings: 'Through the smoke and flame, I gotta go where you are, ba ba-ba-ba-ba ba baaaa . . .'

She comes out of the kitchen with another beautiful brown bottle in her hand, denim shirt all unbuttoned down her front, breasts and Omo-white, her black bra beneath, hair down her neck, bare-legged and laughing. 'What's the nicest thing in the world?'

Jacob sighs and looks at her. 'Well, you, reely.'

She puts the Corbans down and waltzes round the room. 'I'll have the last dance wuth yoo, the last dance togethuh, the last dance wuth yooo . . . Let's have another dry, Jacob, I love you and we'll climb into the kip.'

His heart beats like a haaaaammmer, 'Aaaaaaauuugh, Katus (consults watch but it is still early afternoon) don't know I reely should.'

'Jakob Jakob, a drop of red and into bed.' She sits down beside him and wrinkles her nose. 'I saw God this morning over at the old Cathedral.'

He heaves and stares gloomily at the cast-iron fireplace, stacked with smoking stumps and piles of black coke. 'I'm giving up me present job and going into repertory.'

She stretches her legs to the fire. 'And Jesus was there with all His angels.'

'A few bit parts to start with, then I'm famous.'

'One of the Sisters told me this morning that Father Nolan's got a hernia.'

Jacob looks at her strong, breasty body, Catholic and firmly caloried. 'Do you know what you are?'
'No, what am I?'
'You're my baby-ockle-dockle, ha ha.'
She gets up again from compost heaps of New American paperbacks and piles of newspapers. 'Hey, Jacob, you're bandy.'
'I'm not bandy, I've just got a distinctive walk.'
'And where were you last night?'
'Practising me rep.' He puts on his George Raft raincoat with belt and shoulder buttons and comes toward her. 'You aren't going to like this, babe.'

Thin-lipped, hands in pockets and hair slicked with brilliantine, he swings his fist. Pow. She fiddles with her rusty suspender. Jacob takes off his trench coat and returns from the Simplon Express. 'You know, Katus, I can't make up me mind what I like best—you or me Readers' Digest.'
'Aaaaw, Jacob.'
He smiles evily. 'Let us assume that money is the golden key that opens any door.'
'You've got a grey hair in your side-lever.'
'That, my dear lady, would make you a very rich and very beautiful widow.'
Katie sits on the sofa and takes off her denim. 'Look, I'm going to have a ziz. How's your sister?'
(Omygod) 'I have never seen you looking so loverly. A gownless evening strap. Heh heh.'
'I've bought new unbleached sheets for the bed.'
'Hem haw, reely. Under-reached calico. Um um. I

met a girl in calico, way down in Santa Fe, used to be my Sunday beau before I went awaaaaaay.'
'Jacob, I had a great vision at the Cathedral.'
'And what was that?'
'You, me, and six children, and Father Nolan blessing them.'
'The rep's got far more to offer than bookselling. Fame and fortune, build me bones with Parishes Food and I'll be there. I've been taking elocution lessons without telling you.'
'Father Nolan told me he's found hydatids in his cabbages.'
Jacob fishes in his pocket and takes out one of Aughatane's second-hand pamphlets. Oratory: 'When through the torn sail the wild tempest is streaming, when o'er the dark wave the red lightning is streaking . . .'
'Jacob dalling, how's your glass?'
He raises his legs from the sofa and gazes. 'My thighs are firmer this year.'
'Jaaaaacob?'
'Um? Just up to the top.'
Katie fills his glass, then goes back to the kitchen and surveys the latening afternoon. Outside, the mist is coming down from the black hill where rank kale and turnip grow; she opens the window and hears the cries of the seabirds fighting in stranded seaweed, and the feel of the wind blowing. 'The night is cold, Jacob, the night is cold, and we are growing old, we are growing old.'
He is frightened now and shivers.

'The rep or the Church, Katie, I think I'm basically a religious man. A religious man?'

Kate looks from the hot water tap and comes to the kitchen door, her round stomach showing between T-shirt and skirt.

'Jacob, are you going to wear your trousers rolled?'

'Grow old? Wear my trousers rolled? HAPPY IS THE PEOPLE WHOSE GOD IS THE LORD.'

'Hey, Jacob love,' she calls, 'did I tell you that there's a grey hair in your side-levers?'

Death. Death. 'Dr Joseph Parker said: "There is a mournful tone in this seventh chapter, it is full of disagreeable and dyspeptic remarks, cypress shadows lie over it, Coheleth is in a bilious mood today." *I* am in a bilious mood today, Katie.'

'Where *were* you last night, Jacob?'

'Last night? Sorry about that, Kat. I had to set back to the ranch. The crops are failing. The whole place is in a shambles. Me sister's about to go under a trick-cyclist, Mrs Dolan accidentally swallowed some Phytazol Plant Mixture and Dennis developed a dropped left testicle.'

'Which sister?'

'Um, Edna.'

'Edna?'

Oh Christus. 'Um um um.   Brenda, Brenda, Brenda. If she could get back to her rocks, she'd be okay. (Brilliant) She wants an interest you know. Uncle Albert's (car/donkey/mule/tractor) horse is too old to ride now. Atrophied fetlocks.' He leers with a big Joe E. Brown grin, thousands of teeth

and endless pink gums. 'Gosh, you look naice, Katie, ve'y naice.'
'Have you told them I can help?'
'The first thing I said. Know this fab girl who can cook, work, wash her fingers to the white-meat, look after kinder, but no, no. Proud yeoman's stock is my fambly, proud yeoman's stock. Where are they now, the yeomen of Englaaaaaand?'
'Look love, I'll go up with you later this week.'
'Proud were the bows they bore, when they went off to waaaaaar, dum dum dim dum-dum-dum-dum.'
She has taken off her skirt now and stands thoughtfully by the door in:
T-shirt
(black bra)
pants.
'Do you think,' she says, 'sex before marriage is a sin?'
Jacob, puzzled, has a good look at her little pants and the mount beneath. 'Nah, anytime.'
'But not after you're married.'
'Not at all?'
'Not with other ladies, silly.'
Good grief. 'Nah, that's turrible, turrible (big gnomic Calvin face), a cardinal error.'
'Cardinal Sin.'
'Cardinal Sin.'
Sin. Jacob looks at her again. Long-black-haired, tits bubbing through her Omo T-shirt, milky thighs, curvular mons, and gazes out the window like some ancient mariner, staring across the sea where rain clouds gather.

No little Lord Jesus and His angels,
northwards they have flown from this sky,
dripping rain from perished clouds.
Why does the sparrow stay when he has wings?
'Look, Katus,' he comes up to her, feels her body for an instant and kisses her soft and gentle as a butterfly, 'I'd best be off to McPherson's, then after that Aughie's having a finance committee meeting. It's my turn to be in the chair. Drunk wi' power I am.' He twists his lips and sucks in his cheeks like a north-country mill owner. 'This is not the time, gentlemen, to consider the whims of the individual shareholders, but the future of the company as a whole.' She looks at him and he kisses her soft as fairydown. 'I must be off, Katie the Catholic, but I love you, I love you.'

Bugger bugger, bugger bugger. Jacob stands outside her door, thinks and puts his hand to his head. A fearful cloud is flying. He shoves his hand into his pocket and brings out a Biblecard.

Thoughts For the Day: Animal Series
THE CAMELOPARD
The LORD hath an indictment against Judah and will punish Jacob according to his ways. (Hosea 12, 2.)

11

'Gooday, Jackers. Gooday, Gideon.' Kiss kiss. Tsk tsk. 'You're more than life to me, you're my eternity.' Jacqueline, white-sweatered, stands and looks at her Lochinvar bundling through the door. 'Christ, it's cold, love.' He rubs his hands. 'Freeze the cock off a clothes-peg. Gawd, you're looking nice, I can see your nippos. Where's your bra, pet? Waiting for your lover, ha ha? What's for tea?'

'To what do I owe this, Jacob?'

'What "this"?' He peels a banana and peers in the cot. 'Goodness gracious, Gideon's growing, isn't he? Just like his mother (leer leer) but I do believe there's a bit of the old Dad around the eyes, or is it the mouth? Or is it the nose? Or is it the ears? Or is it the . . . ?'

'This early home, this red letter day?'

'Aw, come off it, Jackers. You want a hard-working man of ambition, don't you?' He pulverises the banana with his teeth, then sucks it with his tongue around the gutters and channels, then swallows. 'Crisis-after-crisis-after-crisis down there these last months, but I'm happy to say at last it's been resolved. Nice bananas.'

'Look, Jacob, the only crisis you know is when the pubs are closed.'

Shit and glumbum. 'Holy mackerel, Jackers, you're in a mood tonight, and I've got great news, great news.'

'What?'

He lays the peel carefully on the boardroom table. 'I've been appointed Managing-Director (Designate).'

'Are you going to leave that there?'

'Eh?'

'That peel. I've just cleaned up. Gorman's coming to dinner.'

'Aw, Christ, I've already seen that fat nit once today at business-man's lunch. When he gets loose in the hospitals there'll be a second bloody black death. God Defend New Zealaaaand.'

'I haven't seen anybody today and he's coming.'

'You'd better go and put a brazeer on then, or are you going to spend the whole night looking like some little went-went girl from a tit show?'

'If you must know, I've just come out of the bath, or that bloody tin that passes for a bath.'

'It's a perfectly good bath. Leaves a few art nouveau impressions on the lumbar regions. Very kinky. Gawd, bare tits in this weather, I don't know how you women do it.'

She looks away and goes into the bathroom.

Ho hum. 'Gooday, Gideon.' Scritch scritch. 'How's

your belly off for fleas? You Dad's just been made heir to a second-hand magazine empire. Have a cigar?' Sniffle snuffle. Sleepy-time grin. 'Up the wooden hill to bed for cheer, laddie's had a long, long day . . .' Jacob sings his little children's song, goes to the window, peels the last banana and considers the world at large. The twinkling lights are on all over Flagstaff town. From Marie Byrd Land comes this wind that blows. The sun is drowned in the night, and from the rattling branch, black pine-cones fall below to the narrow road of stone where the ragwort grows. No eye this night upon the sparrow where he sleeps in the ruined crib of stone. Jacob leans out the window and hears the two women talking in the garden beneath.

'Oooooooooooow, these should make a nice display in the front, Mrs M.'
'What are they, dear?'
'Hyacinth. White Lady. Lovely white.'
'Yeeeees?'
'And Hyacinth. Queen of the Pinks. Lovely bright rosy pink.'
'They sound nice.'
'And rununculas. Austral Giants. Famous Australian strain.'
'They sound nice.'
The sod is turned and the grass grubs wriggle.
Jacob sticks his head out into the gathering gloom. 'Why don't you try Lord Balfour's Choice, Lovely Mauve?'
Windy silence.
'Or some Regal Pelargoniums? Midget Ageratums?

Mesembryantheums? Dwarf Patagonian Fartoniums? They make a nice spring show.'
His wife is back fully clothed. 'Jacob, I've got to live with those two even if you don't.'
'I'm just giving the old Southern share-croppers a few suggestions, love. I wouldn't mind a few Spring Fartoniums growing on the old outside dunny.' He makes toward the door.
'And where are you going now?'
'Goin' out ta feed me banties.'
'Those bloody hens. They never lay any eggs and you don't look after them properly.'
'Eggs? One laid an egg yesterday.'
'Where is it then?'
'And I do look after them. I gave them some budgie seed this morning. They lapped it up. Kawk kawk.'
'Where's the egg?'
'Choice scraps, leftover angel cake, pavlova, old fly cemeteries, Yorkshire pud, the lot.'
'I never make Yorkshire pudding.'
'No, but Aughie does. And kindly gives me pieces to take home for the banties.'
'Oh God, you're lying as usual.'
'Me lie about Aughie's Yorkshire pud? Hot gospel. He's a master at it. Keeps him going all winter long.'
'I don't know why I ever let you buy those bloody hens. That's one thing I *haven't* got against Mrs Miffawney.'
'That menopausic old bitch. I'm reporting her to the R.S.P.C.A. for cruelly treating me banties and feeding them poisoned bread and butter custard.'

'What's she done to your wretched birds? She just wants them out on account of hygiene, and I don't blame her. Bloody filthy things.'
'And I've seen you down there late at night with meno Miffawney, scaring the daylights out of the little creatures.'
'What rot.'
'I've seen you. And you pinch the eggs on the sly.'
'I've told you before. I haven't seen an egg for months.'
'They've been laying.'
'Where are they then?'
'I've taken them all to work.'
'What for?'
'For Aughie to put in his Yorkshire pudding.'
'Look, Jacob, you might as well know now. Life with you is becoming absolutely impossible.'
'Aw, Jackers.'
'You don't seem to have the drives of normal, responsible men.'
'Drives? I've got drives I haven't driven yet and you've had orgasms to prove it.'
'Business drives, career drives. When are you going to stop mucking around and playing the fool? When are you going to earn a decent living and support me like any other man. When?'
Lummee, the shrill-pitched voice and tears not far away.
'Jesus Christ, I've just been made Managing-Director. What more do you want?'
'Bloody rubbish. A bankrupt second-hand bookshop

in a bankrupt town. Your pay's been doubled for your new responsibilities no doubt?'
'Just a sec, Jackers, that was a banty squawk. (Do ventriloquist act from side of mouth) Bet one's laid an egg. They've all laid eggs and those two old bints will pinch them. You can make soufflé for tea. Back in a jiff.'
Bang, click, bang.

Jacquie, Jacob and Gorman. Her dinner is eaten and the sofa is occupied. Jacob probes with a toothpick he has found in his pocket. 'Well, Gorman, it's good to have ye aboard.' Silence. 'I was with me hens just before you arrived and one of them's got what looks like parasitic nodules on her feet. You couldn't have a look after coffee, could you?'
'That's more of a job for a vetenarian don't you think, Jacob?'
'Aw, I don't know. They're almost human, my birds. And our budgie's been a bit crook too. What about taking a dekko at that while you're on the job?'
'I'm sure Gorman doesn't find you funny, Jacob. Why must you denigrate everything that's worthwhile?'
'Denigrate? Blimey, I'm serious, my love. Where would we be without our little feathered friends? They're all God's creatures. You've taken the Hippocratic oath haven't you, Gorms?'
'Not yet, Jacob, not yet.'
'Cut me legs off and call me Shorty. I thought you blokes took Hippo's oath before entering the portals. I'd better see the Vice-Chancellor about that.'

'Gorman dear, have some more sherry.' Jacqueline bends and passes the bottle.

Gorman dear? Uuuuuuuurrrgh. 'Well the best you can do is to get me some cut-price Bob Martins when next you're down at the dispensary, and while you're there I'll have some Tibs Round Worm tablets and a hundred anti-mate pills. Have some after-dinner nougat?'

'Jacob,' snarl snarl, 'you're not funny, just bloody disgusting. Just because Gorman's making more of his life than you are.'

Gorman puffs. 'I wouldn't say that, Jacqueline, but as the French say, "Chacun à son gout." '

Chacun à son gout? 'By jove, Gorman, I think I see a bertie-germ burrowing into your left follicule, or is it fullicule? You's better get that removed before you go into Surgery tomorrow morning. Blackheads left in the old incision, worse than your handkerchief, tut tut.'

Gorman removes his glasses, takes out his pipe and plunges.

'What's this big financial deal you were discussing at lunchtime, Jacob?'

'That was a definite squawk. Old bitcho's down there again.'

His trouble-and-strife flexes her breasts once more. 'What financial deal?'

'Jesus, did you hear that? Another squawk.' He gets up and cranes his head out the window. 'Ahem, any good prods at the Medical School this week, Gorms? Or do you reserve yourself for the female patients?

Look, if you'll excuse me for a sec, I'll just hop downstairs and see what meno Miffawney's doing to me birds.' Jacob heaves the sound of a thousand sighs and disappears.

Gorman watches Jacob go, then stuffs half a pound of Hollandia Aromatic into his imported Meerschaum.
'Do you think he knows?'
'Gorman, Jacob is so full of himself he wouldn't know if we were doing it in front of him.'
Gorman shakes and, like an over-weight Sindbad, lumbers to his feet and tries to find his bearings in this darkening, windy night. No moon in the sky where the cypresses bend and blow, the coke fire splutters and the old logs dry and peel. He looks at her leg and thigh again, the suspender button and the little knob of nylon. The budgie wakes and croaks, the curtains flutter sadly and the clock ticks. Phut? Phat? Sut? Plat?

'Gooday, gooday, all the birds are sleeping in their nests, Mrs Miffawney's reading a 1953 *Picture Post* and God is in his heaven. Very cold, very cold. Freeze the pubics off a cast-iron post it would.'
Gorman starts loading up his gear, Parker pen and pencil set, spare pipe stem, long-range glasses, tobacco pouch, prodder/tamper, close-range glasses, paperback copy of Harold Robbins, anti-wind butane pipe-lighter.
'You aren't going now are you, Gorman? You've forgotten your spare leather arm-patches, your matching

set of condoms *à la Japonaise*, your *Black's Medical Dictionary*. Come again sometime, come again.'
Gorman strides purposefully behind the sofa and kisses the back of her fair neck. 'Goodnight, Jacqueline dear. Thank you for such a nice dinner. Jacob.'
'Golly Moses, it's early-times yet, Gorman. Goonight. Goodnight.'
She rises from the couch and sees him to the door. 'Goodnight, Gorman (touch touch), goodnight.'

The wooden castle creaks and sounds drift through the open window.
'I think we'll miss these hydrangeas, Mrs M.
   Mrs M?'
The woodwork cracks on the rococo verandah.
'Lovely, dear, lovely.'
Somewhere a radio plays and Jacob listens to the band of eventide.
Abiiiiiiiiiiiiide with meeeeeee, da da da da, daa-daa.
'A nice chap Jackers, but a bit heavy around the old tree stumps.'
She moves toward the dishes. 'God, I get ashamed of you Jacob.'
'Ashamed? Jumping Jesus, you spent all night pissing in each other's pockets. Jellybeans wouldn't melt in your ovaries. Watch out for Gorman, my love, he's got a head shaped like a shaggy condom and a John Thomas that sprays foaming jelly. A real sly bastard, I know his type. If you bent over a bucket, you'd find his dork up your Godiva.'

'God,' she crashes the dishes, 'you're disgusting.'
'Look, Jackers, just remember Grimsdyke in *Doctor in the House*, I know, I know.'
'You ruined the dinner after all I went to.' Sniff sniff.
'Aw, come on, Jackers, you're luvly without your brazeer, all tit and cashmere.' He comes up behind her. 'Titty-poo, titty-poo, yum yum.'
'I can't stay with you, I really can't.'
'Stay with me? Of course you can (tremble tremble) I love you, I love you, I love you.'

But the fire is going out, and across the valley comes the sound of bagpipes playing.
Will ye no come back again?

'Ah-ah-ah all of mee, wh-wh-wh-why not take all of mee . . . ?' Old-coated, scarved to the ankles and singing to himself, Jacob comes down Mr Boldini's curving staircase and runs his lucky penny along the grooves in the teak banisters. 'Ca-ca-ca-can't yooo see ah-ah-ahm no good wuthout yooo . . . ?'

Plastic teatrays and old cracked cups, bang, bang, Mrs Miffawney toils along the corridor, crooked in the seam, cold in the twat and creased up the bum. Jacob hides and clutches his figleaf as she passes and disappears into the PRIVATE. Coff coff. He stands and peers in her upstairs parlour. The stag is still at bay and the mountains weep. He sniffs at the dead hydrangeas crumbling on the upright piano. Oooooooooow, these dried flower-arrangements always make a nice display. An historic place. Old *Picture Posts* and *Auckland Weeklies*, maiden hair fern in brass tureens, yellow gondolas on orange canals. Lovely. Lovely. 'Yew took the porut that once wus mah horut, so why not take aaaaaaaal of meeeee.'
The wind blows and the venetians rattle. An old relic

of halcyon boardinghouse days: PLEASE TURN OFF THE LIGHT WHEN VACATING THE ROOM. He turns it on and shuts the door.

'Goodmorning, Mr Small.' (He has paid the rent, *ergo* she speaks.)
'Gooday, Mrs M. I must say those aggies make a nice show.' She is carrying an old G.E.C. electric jug and a peeling Speedie toaster to brown the bread and make the tea. Her cords dangle and the kitchen door closes. The S.T.C. mantel is switched on to THE RADIO CHURCH OF THE HELPING HAND and an egg is boiled. A piece of toast for the budgie, Jacob moves stealthily and peers through her keyhole. Sounds of Oral Roberts and THE LITTLE CHAPEL OF GOOD CHEER, but nothing to be seen. Ho hum, what is there without faith and the song that brings us happiness?

In the garden, a warm breeze blows. Jacob looks toward Mount Cargill, and then the long peninsula, and dreams of the great pleasure gardens, where once the miners danced and sang and lay with golden courtesans in shady grottoes, where Chinese lanterns shone by crystal pavilions of glittering glass, rococo spires and beds of fuchsias, mountain lilies and broad-leafed trees. All was shouts and German bands, bars and fireworks high and flying in the southern sky where the miners rode proudly on the coach and thumped their heavy bags of gold that spilt like sand across the wooden counter.

'Areyouthere?' Mrs Dolan calls. 'Mrs Miffawney, are youthere?'

The wind smells of snow again while the early service church bells ring. The hills are blue and black and white, and smoke is on this breeze, spinning as it goes. The trees are shining as crickets sing in lumps of catmint and spiky hawthorn trees. The sun is shining too, and stuccoed houses gleam by cliffs of rock where supplejack and creeper grow across the red and grainy stones. In the park, the glasshouse glitters by gardenseats and oaks, slides and swings and fairytrees. The thrushes' nest is empty in the wild and rambling hedge. Jacob makes his way through the park, across the rustic bridge, dawdles by the polyanthus beds, walks straight through the maze, around the Shakespeare garden, between the black, large-leafed gunneras, makes a wish by the wishing-well, through the wicket gate and out into George Street. He decides to buy some Kool Mints down at McDee's.

'Gooday, Cheryl, a bit of snow about, eh? How's your Kool Mint stock?'
'Hullo, Jacob.' She grins at him over her counter as he eyes her charlies sticking through her sweater.
'I thought I might drop around tonight and shout you a drink.'
She runs her tongue over her teeth. 'Ooooooooo, that'll be nice.' Their cold fingers touch.
'Hullo, Jacob.'
He wheels around like Wyatt Earp to see Kate

Donahue standing there as large as life. 'Aaaaaaaaaah, gooday, Katharine, gooday. I was just saying to Miss McLennan here, it looks like snow. By Jove, yes.' Weather-beaten face of trawler fisherman in the North Atlantic. The wind machine moans, he screws up his eyes and raises his index finger toward the ceiling. 'I'm pretty good at it you know. Almost uncanny. It was I who predicted the great snow of '66. Well, ladies, time is money and I've got a plane to catch.' He leaves the shop, strides purposefully past the window, stops and peers back in through the Rothman's showcards. Katie is buying her cigarettes, fishes into her suede Maid Marian coin bag and stops as Cheryl's fat lips move. Good grief. He stares, lip-reads madly and rushes back inside. 'Gooday, Katus, have-you-got-a-minute?' He takes her arm and drags her from the shop. 'Cripes, I've just remembered me back, ooooooooooaaaaaaaaaah.' He puts his hands on his kidneys. 'Eeeeeeeeee, it's agony, can you do anything?'
'Look, Jacob, what can I do now? I'm due at the hospital in five minutes. That girl seems to know you pretty well, doesn't she?'
Omygod. 'Knowmewell? She's mad, nutty as a fruitcake, typically frustrated spinster. I can never get away from her, a case for treatment if you ask me. Ooooooooaaaaaah.'
'She's hardly over nineteen.'
'All the signs of hysterical pregnancy, man-grabber, hand-holder, Freudian spider syndrome, destined for the psychiatric wards, tut tut. What about me back?'
'You'll have to wait until tonight. Here's my bus.'

He stands sagging. Good grief. Where are the sunny breasted girls floating spindle-heeled on copper-coloured days? Good grief. Bumarooskie, has the shit really hit the fan, as the saying goes?

Jacob mooches gloomily down George Street and enters Aughatane's. Mr Doomsbury is coming out, wearing slouch hat and baggy whipcords, his bowie-hangs trailing in the dirt. 'Gooday, Mr Doomsbury, a bit of snow about? It's comin' over the old Inangahua Mountains. Can't you feel it in your bones?'
'Sheep four feet high they was.'
'It's comin' in from the wild and woolly Lammerlaws like the big freeze of '66. My Gawd, yes.'
Mr Doomsbury stops and points his aged weathervane south to Princes Street and crumbling packs of ice. 'Four feet high they was and Shorty laid them down gently as a lamb.' He clutches his leather bound *History of the Penoponnesian Wars* under his arm and heads for the Public Library.
'It doesn't open until ten,' Jacob calls, but Mr Doomsbury has gone between early-morning buses, bread vans and dust carts.

Inside, all is still. Smells of pamphlets, provincial incunabula, unknown books and old stew. 'Mr Aughatane? Mr Aughatane? (plummy tones) my name is Harris-Tweed and I'm calling on behalf of Southebys'.' Silence. 'Ahem, I've been told your Bertha Ruck Collection is worth a fortune.' Jacob adjusts his trilby hat, lights a hand-made Dunhill and waits.

'Good morning, Mr Small. Heh heh. I thought I heard your voice. I liked the look of your lady friend.' The wind blows up his pipe as he adjusts his paper collar and stands, hands in gaping pockets. Fiddle-dee-dee with the cockatoo this bright and ballsy morning. 'It looks like snow, Mr Aughatane. Our esteemed colleague, Mr Doomsbury, predicts the first fall at a quarter past four.'

Aughatane takes his teeth from the peanut butter glass, pops them in, wipes his nose on a spare collar and stands ready for the day. 'Someone, Mr Small, has taken a Beatrice Harradin and a box of Biblecards. We'll have to take the stock before the week is out.' Moly Hoses, collapsing condoms, take stock of this bloody book emporium? *The Scots' Worthies, Walks in Maoriland Byways, Angels of Light, Heaven's Morning Breaks—An Anthology of the Afterlife?* 'Quite so, Mr Aughatane, quite so.' Jacob whips out his short-hand notebook, shoves a biro behind his ear and busies around the shelves. Aughatane goes over to his art collection and pokes at the folders: *The Violin Practice* (brings tears to the eye) a complete set of matching Cruickshank engravings (original copies, priceless, priceless):

January: *New Year's Eve*
February: *Transfer Day at the Bank*
March: (missing)
April: (missing)
May: *All a-growing*
June: (missing)
July: *Down at Beulah*

August: (missing)
Deep in darkness, Jacob reads *Tried Recipes* by Bertha Rickerby.
'Yew took the porut that once was mah horut, so why not take aaaaaaal of meeeeee?'

The clock strikes six, it is snowing and the town is beautiful. So white, so white, sweet snow falls this soft black night on old villas sleeping in embroidered dressing gowns. Dogs bark, dogs bark, and children shout in this town of black and white, where the snow is soft to tread and sweet to suck from the dark, green leaf. A child's Christmas Eve this night of late July. Now the snow is on the vine and the blue convolvulus. Hoary icicles glitter on fence-posts, trees and drains, while old men leave their darkened rooms and laugh for all the young and white of it, as snow is falling on the childish face. The clock tower chimes this white and silver time, and all this night the town will sleep, soft and clean in its little bed.

'Jesus, look at the snow, Cheryl me love, ain't it marvellous?' Jacob takes a Brandy Vino so he can be in Panama, Guatemala or Brazil. The Bowling Green Hotel, painted glass and old walnut, cherubims and cherubums carefully crafted eighty years ago, jars of Antarctic oysters and jellied pigs' cheeks, bottles of Guinness and foaming tubes of Dominion Bitter. Hip-up-close she stands, Evening in Paris poured in all her cracks, pearls around her neck, patterned panti-hose covering her shanks, she feels her winter oats this

snowy evening. 'Hoo was that girl this morning, Jacob?'
'Have a jellied pig's cheek, love.'
'Hoo was that girl?'
He feels her beefy, young thighs, raised in pasture where the hay was yellow and sweet, and passes her a Wicked Lady to warm up her flesh and tickle the juice that flows in her tubes. 'A client, a client, I'm going into publishing and she's writing a book on bones. Make a fortune down at the Medical School.'
I'll buy yooo a diamond ring, any-thing . . .
'She seemed to know you very well.'
Where have I heard that before? Never give your right name, no,no,no. 'You're looking ve'y naice tonight, ve'y naice.' He runs his thumb under her mini. 'What's the drive-men-crazy perfume, love?'
She pops in a pickled pig's cheek. 'Evening in Paris, old man McDee gets it wholesale, do you want to smell it?'
Uuuuuuuuuuurrrgh. 'Weeeeel, I go for you wholesale.'
Tickle-ickle.
'Do yooo?'
'Ah dooo.'
She rubs her tits down his front. 'Back in a tick, just going to the Ladies.'

'Same again please, George, I'm as dry as a lizard tonight.'
Whisky and milk, rum and lemon, stubbies of export beer, the bar is packed this winter night. The beer

tubes pump and the organolium plays hit tunes of long, long ago, as the overcoated crowd presses Jacob against the bar. Silver threads among the gold, he suddenly sees Gorman approaching and starts to struggle madly, but cannot get out. Through the crowd the bearded body draws nearer and nearer, Jacob turns a blank back and stares steadily at bottles of Dewars, Lemon Heart and Gilbeys, but finally he feels a heavy hand on his shoulder and the familiar voice speaks.
'Hullo, Jacob.'
'Greetings, Gorman, ha ha, long-time-no-see. Just having one on me own at the end of a long day, but must be off to me loved ones, hem haw.'
Gorman takes his time and gropes escapologist for his pipe concealed somewhere in his tweeds, then moors alongside.
'I've just left Urinary-Digestion, I didn't think I'd see you this time of night.'
'Urinary-Digestion? By Jove. Look, Gormo, have a preserved eel, very tasty, but must be off, must be off. Pleasant to see you but time's a-wasting.' Now, from the corner of his eye, he sees his Queen of the Plough approaching, and like a young heifer struggling in the stalls, Cheryl draws near her bale of hay.
'Ooooooooooooooh, hullo Mr Gorman, fancy seeing you here, how are you? Can I have another drink, Jacob darling?'
'Christ, a terrific juke box here, all the old favourites, there's a shanty in old shaaaaaaaanty toooooooooown, ba ba ba boo boo, you're up and down . . .'
Gorman squints.

'. . . a little old shack by the railroad track . . .'
Cheryl gets up close and wraps her fat lips around his ear.
'Another drinkie?'
'. . . that's the shanty in oooooooooooold Shanty Toooooooooooown. George, George (goodgod) another drink if you pulease.'
Cheryl clenches her stubby fingers amongst his. 'Jacob lent me such a spicy book, Mr Gorman, *Forever Amber*, have you read it? A naughty on every page, so he said.'
Jacob raises his eyes heavenward. Who is this girl? Who is she?
'Mind you, he could have written it himself, tee hee.'
She runs her pink tongue around her glass, burps and slides her meaty arm around Jacob's palpitating waist. 'Cold outside, Mr Gorman, but nice in here intit?'
Gorman carefully prods his pipe and strokes his Mustapha beard. 'It was very nice to run into you Jacob, and Cheryl. I've got to be back at Casualty at seven.'
Jacob plays his last card. 'By Jove, you two are pretty friendly, ha ha. I've seen you both swapping drinkies at the Tasman. Very close. I've got to go now, but I bet you'd like to be alone tonight . . .' But aromatic at full blast, Gorman has flexed his mighty muscles and disappeared between sou'westers, balaclavas, steaming raincoats, hand-knit hats and vacant umbrellas. Cheryl sighs. 'Such a nice man, Jacob, but not so nice as yoo.'
'Yeh, his blood's worth bottling. Shan't be a minute,

nature calleth, back in a jiff, save me another, see ya shortly.' Goonight, goonight, goonight all, goonight.

Outside, Jacob stands and shivers beneath the sleeping tree. The moon is ice as it hangs from the southern sky. The Southern Cross is slowly wheeling with its constellation, the oak is bare, and in the slender leaves of grass, the dew is hardening into frost that soon will glitter when this night is through. Smoke from winter fires and battered chimney-pots gathers, gathers, and chokes the throat of this town. From the sky, soot is falling on the lone white flower like black and poisonous snow, the birds are cold and blue tonight. Over the hills and far away in the soundless hinterland, snow is falling on the high and ragged peaks, driving the sheep, the mountain goat and the frightened deer down the slopes to the lower reaches where the beech and aspen grow by mossy streams and ruined huts. The musterer is gone, the mountain hawk is dead and Flagstaff is going to sleep.

Tomorrow when the sun is up, hawthorn trees will dance and sing, and tiny streams will flow through silver grass. But in the night, black blood will flow down secret drains and rain will fall upon the bone, buried in its grave of grey and bitter stone.

'9½lb OF COCOANUT ICE,' Alf McDermott cries, 'TWO HAND-CARVED POT-STANDS, A SET OF BILLIARD BALLS, GODBLESS ALL OUR RADIO-LISTENERS TODAY. YOU'RE MORE THAN LIFE TO ME YOU'RE MY ETERNITY, (LOWER THE SCREEN SANDY IF YOU PLEASE) DOO DOO DEE DOO DA DA DOO.'
Jacob and Katie sit at the back of the Flagstaff Lower Town Hall, holding hands and listening to the quivering, cracked old voices.
'What on earth are we doing here at the Community Sing, Jack?'
'Flah thuh ocean in a silvah puhlane, see the jungool when it's wet wuth rahain, we're singing, at least I am. I thought you'd like a good sing, Katus, it drives the blues away. They'll do some Irish numbers and you'll be jerking dew-drops all ovah thuh puhlace.'
'You aren't singing the right song.'
'Oh yes I am. I had a chat with Alf McDermott on the way in and he wants me to sing counterpoint.'

'You're on with that girl at the barber's aren't you?'
'Aaand remembuh when yoooo're home aghain yoo buhlong tuh meee. What girl?'
'The fat one. Cheryl McSomething-or-other.'
'Gawd, there's some good stuff going today. These Sings are where you get the bargs and it all goes to a Good Cause.'
'A VERY GENEROUS BID FOR THE SIX BANTY HENS (COFF COFF) AND TEN BOB FROM AUNTY SISSIE'S MOTHER'S GIRL FROM RAVENSBOURNE.'
'Crikey, Kate, Alf's got some banties today, if I had ten-and-six I'd . . .'
'Well it's not as if we're married or anything.'
'SIX BREAD-BAGS AND TWO HAND-MADE MOP-HEADS SO GENEROUSLY DONATED, (LOWER THE SCREEN ONCE AGAIN SANDY IF YOU PLEASE).'
'Cheryl McDoonville? You must be joking.' He turns to her in his creaking seat and adopts the 1938 Hollywood approach. 'I never saw that girl before in my life.'
'WHEN YOU'VE GOT FRIENDS AND NEIGHBOURS THE WORLD'S A HAPPIER PLACE, WHEN YOU'VE GOT FRIENDS AND NEIGHBOURS AND A SMILE A-PON YOUR FACE.'
'How long have you known her?'
'Look, Kate, that's a veery nice set of hand-embroidered wagon covers.'
'How long?'

'Gawd, I don't *know* her, I just buy me cheroots there because it's close to the shop.'

'THREE BOOT-SCRAPERS MADE FROM BOTTLE-TOPS, REPRESENTS HOURS OF WORK FROM GOODYTWOSHOES OF POINT MCCULLOUCH. DOODEE DOO DOO TIDDLY BOM BOM YOU'RE THE WEALTHIEST MAN IN TO-OWN.'

'She seems to know you pretty well.'

Christus, where *have* I heard that before? 'Look, I told you, she's a man-grabber. What do they call those sticky South American plants that catch flies and snakes and bats? She's one of those. Anyway, what about my aching back?'

'RAINHAT MADE FROM FLOUR-BAG, GENEROUSLY SENT BY A WEE ADMIRER OF HARRY LAUDER (GODBLESS HIM) AT HAGGERTY'S BAY. THERE'S A LONG LONG TRAIL A-WINDING LA LA LA LA LAA LAA LAA LAA . . .'

'Well that's that Kate, and a very good Sing too. Ol' Alf really takes the biscuit for the lunchtime show. I'd have given me eye teeth for those banties, the ones I've got now are all clucky.'

Kate links her arm through his as they move with the crowd toward the big oak doors. 'I didn't know you kept hens, Jacob.'

'Weeel, I don't reely, it's me sister Eileen. Bit of a hobby.'

'I thought it was Edna.'

'That's what I said, Edna.'

'But didn't you once say, Brenda?'
'Yep, that's what I once said, Brenda. Always get confused, my sister Eileen died in childbirth.'
'That must have been sad for your mother.'
'Nah, Mum's been passed on for many a season. Eileen conked having Reggie.'
'Who looks after him then?'
'Aw, Reggie takes it in turns. Nice little fella but only eighteen-and-six in the pound. Bit of a worry to us all. Gooday, Alf, a very nice show.'
In the street, all is Christmas Day and white. Kate suddenly stops and looks at him with her deep river-blue eyes. 'You know, Jacob, you're a very strange man. A very strange man.'
'Me strange? Ha ha ha.' They stand in the snow, blowing steam.
'You're a lovely loving man, but I don't believe a word you tell me. You know that, don't you?' A few gentle snowflakes fall and settle in her long black hair as she stands firm and beautiful in the snow. He looks at her, and in the Town Hall the old electric organ still plays sad and familiar melodies. 'Aw, Ka-ka-katie,' he shivers and trembles, 'I'll walk you up the hill. Alfred Doomsbury's got the shop for the afternoon.'

Side by side and silent, they walk up Stuart Street and climb above the town. Past the overgrown Norman masonry of Flagstaff Boys' High School they go, then they stop to look at their cold, clear, provincial world.

'Look, Katie,' Jacob cries, 'look, the sky is blue today.'

Blue is the sky this day, as blue as the sea where white clouds swim and tumble in this cool and gentle breeze, and toss the silver sun from slopes of snow that blind the joyous eye. On Mount Cargill, Silver Peak, Mount Murchison and Halfway Bush, all the world's tobogganing on slopes clean and white and sheer, where crystal drifts are piled high beneath a thousand Christmas trees, tinkling twinkling ice that spins silver glass and baubles gleam and shine cold and beautiful. Laugh and shout, school's out, school's out, and all the children play and slide down snow-sloped hills by manuka, oak and pine. Stout brown boots, corduroys, woollen pompomed hats and fairisle gloves, they scream and laugh and glissade on appleboxes, old tin trays, sledges and skis, tumble tumble, all is silver ice and snow by the snowman standing proud and grinning for all the fun of it.

The Town Hall clock chimes and childs' voices rise through the fragile air. Jacob and Kate, cold and clean and blowing steam, trudge on up the hill to Southey Street beneath the quiet trees and weatherbeaten terrace houses. Snow is on the dovecote on the lawn, snow is on the iron roof and in the copper spouting, snow is in the blackbird's nest and on the rock where the beetles live, snow is on the spire and the parapet, snow is on the cross of stone and in the ruined sepulchre, snow is on the tops of posts and chimney-pots, snow is on the towpath winding on the hill, in the grass and liverwort, in the gorse and hawthorn tree, in the gully where the morepork sleeps, in the quarry and the limestone pit, in the cracks upon the path, snow is on the stacks of hay, in the woolshed, on the piles of coke and coal where the goods trucks stand. Now all is breath and leaves of ice as cars and trucks and buses climb with chains upon the hill where the workmen throw black gravel on the white and gleaming road.

Jacob looks and laughs. He bends and makes a snowball and smashes it hard against the fence. Honey for the bellbird, the waxeye and the tui, fresh bread for the sparrows and the pigeons as they fly and flutter from the icy chandelier, sparkling bright and wonderful. The sun is low and brown ducks fly across this winter season.

Katie's door, stained glass, snow on the step and icicles dripping. Jacob hesitates as she fishes in her bag for the key. 'Can I come in?' he asks, 'can I come in?'
'Of course you can, silly.'
The door closes behind them and she hangs up her snowy old coat, unties her hair, pulls back the curtains, sits down and takes off her boots. 'Jacob,' she says, warm inside, sprawled on the sofa, the coal fire still burning, 'what do you intend to do?'
Intend to do? 'Um um (he is cold deep, ice fills his heart and his frigid lungs are pumping) Aughie's shop is worth a fortune, one good sale, clean out the shit

and we're home and hosed. Golly Moses Kate, the stock there is fabulous. The other day I came across a 1923 edition of Clarence E. Mulford's *Hopalong Cassidy*. Incredible.'

'What do you believe in, Jacob?'

'Oh Gawd, I dunno.' He looks out of her window to see fresh snow falling? 'What about a drink, Kate? What do *you* believe in?'

'You know, Jacob: Jesus Christ, and the Holy Mother of God, and all the Saints, and the Confession and Father Nolan. What about you?'

He drinks deeply on his Amontillado Dry, grabs the poker and roots at the fire burning and crumbling in the grate. 'Um um, the wind and the snow, spiders, fish, whales, old dotty trees, moss and stones, forgotten books, women like you, the Lammerlaw Mountains, lumpy hills, opossums, pigeons and the seasons, the seasons.'

'Why include women like me?'

'Ah, you're a bit of rock and tree and ice and bird and mountain flower, Katie.'

She leans and kisses him on his forehead. 'I know now why you tell all those lovely stories.'

'Stories? Stories? Honest Injun, Kate, I don't tell stories. Stories, no. Can I tickle your thigh before you fly away to the mountains?'

She leans and kisses him again. 'You may, you may.'

He does.

'I remember,' she says, staring far away, 'my father ploughing, year after year with the horses and the river flowing, and the river flowing, and my mother and father and six brothers and the ploughing. Each winter it would snow for two or three months, great snowfalls from the Alps and the little birds I had fed all spring and summer would die, but there were my father and mother and my six brothers ploughing.'

'Why did you leave, Kate?'

'Too tough, Jacob, too tough. All that work on that hard land and sometimes bad seasons. My mother used to make big fruitcakes for the men, big ten pound cakes, stuffed with raisins, currants and dates, soaked in wine and covered with marzipan. Then, laden with baskets, she would walk three or four miles over the stubbled paddocks, through the post and wire gates and over the bridges to the men sweating in the insulage pits, where the green grass was packed and buried for feed during the long, cold winter. All that work and death and the terrible change of seasons. The south wind it blew, and when my father died my mother didn't know what to do so she followed him. My father's funeral was the biggest in Bannockburn, ha ha, a Catholic farmer being R.I.P.'d in a Scottish town. You feed the birds don't you, Jacob? You've told me?'

'Aye, I do.'

'Well, God's going to take them away, all away where the south wind blows.'

'Tell me, Kate, is it possible to love everything?'

'Aye, Jack, it's possible, but just remember everything won't love you back. An old tree you have once loved can be a tricky and dangerous thing. It's possible, but I remember my father's plough used to break

sometimes on the stumps of old trees. How's your glass?'
They both sit very still, breathing and thinking alone as the clock ticks and the outside wind starts to blow.
'Katus?'
'Um?'
'What about to bed, to bed to rest our head?'
'No, Jacob, no, I don't think so. I don't think so.'
'Why?' he says, knowing the answer and not looking at her but staring away like a bird hovering over the white roof tops. 'Why?'
'It's not the time any more.'
'I'd best be getting back then.'
She looks at him. 'Aye, you'd best.'
Kate helps him into his coat, kisses him lightly on the cheek (did he feel it?) and the door closes.

Sadness, sadness, I have deceived a young Catholic girl and there is no health in me. The blue sky has gone and great grey clouds are rolling across the late and windy afternoon. What'll I doo when yoo are far away, what'll I doo, what'll I doo, what'll I doo?
Tortoise-like and deep in his coat, Jacob walks through the grey and dirty snow across town.

14

Still and snow. Still and snow. Black smoke winds from ten thousand chimney pots this late day. At St Clair and St Kilda, the beach is white and the rocks are covered with snow and ice. Strange snow on sand and the birds are silent. One lone cormorant flies.

On the waterfront at Marine Parade, flanked and fortressed by old Victorian boardinghouses, Jacob sits on a council seat, donated by Angus McFee 1908 (TO HIS MEMORY), pooped and pockmarked, and never known spurting lovers. The big tidal swimming pool is empty, the playground is silent, motionless swings and roundabouts, rusted metal slides (where are the children's cries?) and on the hill the shattered glasshouse waits for cloudless, cloudless skies. (Arica, Iquique, Antofagasta, Santiago, Conception.) Ruined cupolas and canals unbuilt, the Doges have died, ROCKY LOVES BEV 1941, the iron rusts and stains the snow, LADIES GENTS, the cistern is dry and full of cold sand, ONIONHEAD LOVES K.T. The two-storied houses stand sightless against the sea, their holland blinds and wormy venetians ghostly moving and tapping against the pane. Nothing stirs in the narrow sandy streets of cardboard houses, wizened gardens and painted corner shops. TIP TOP ICE-CREAM, FLAGSTAFF DAILY TIMES, BIRDSEYE FROZEN FOODS, pennysuckers, Throaties, Sunshine Soup. Plastic shopping baskets on counters cold. A winter seaside town where the coal smoke never rises and hovers forever in the valley. Jacob turns and gazes toward the hill. Would that he were in the mountains, the Rock and Pillar Range, the Dunstans, Rough Ridge, the Hawkduns, the dreadful McKerrows, falling sheer with tiny footholds only for ice and snow to the sprawling, shingly Hunter River. Baloo My Boy, this gentle wind is cold as it blows from the South Pacific Sea.

Back along King Edward Street toward town Jacob walks. A thoroughfare of disused tram-tracks and wounded trolley buses, the smell of coal gas and soot; big, young, overcoated women pushing children in carts, their seams are crooked and their shoe-heels split. Wheezing they stand, pebble-lensed and podded, breathing on shop windows, bunny-wool gumboots and coats to the ankles. It is the three o'clock matinée and the children run through the dirty snow to the Regal Cinema and stand in shaking queues. Oooooooooooh, coloured lights and sweetstands, the Circus is Coming, patchwork marquees and donkey rides across deserted stony lots. Under the coats, the young childish shoulders bend as the wind starts to blow and cold cinders fly. THE LORD CAN MAKE

MORE WITH YOUR LIFE THAN YOU CAN.
The cinema doors open and the children move inside
to darkness, tired seats and old delights on baking
Western plains.

Jacob stands in front of the Regal and remembers
Charles Starrett, Buck Jones and Andy Devine, the
horses, the mesas and the mountains, the mountains
where he was born by the raw and streaming river,
where as a child he used to play, the high alpine
meadows, red-berried in the autumn with secret
ditches and narrow drains. Where did the big brown
trout rise? Over the shifting shingle flats and in the
silent, weedy backwaters of the high-country river.
Standing there, he remembers the small brick and
board towns, where post and rail fences fell, where
mine shafts crumbled, old trees staggered and puzzled
little lambs died, waiting and bleating for the spring
that hid behind the mountain.

He pauses by the Salvation Army Hall. (What do you
intend to do, Jacob? What do you believe in?) General
Booth is dead, the windows are barred, the door is
nailed shut, no band plays *Salute the Happy Morn.
Eileen Aroon? The Blue Juanita? Songs My Mother
Taught Me?*

Afternoon, Charlie. Afternoon, Gladys . Afternoon,
George. Coff coff. Mind the trolley-bus. Beneath the
boots and home-made shopping trundlers, the snow is
turning grey and black, and by the gasworks, the

furnaces glow. Coke in giant piles for suburban stoves.
COOK WITH GAS. By the front gates elephantic
backsides bend as old women collect firewood from
mossy piles of dank lumber. Rusting bedsprings that
will never burn, empty letter boxes, cardboard tubes,
they pick through the timber from wrecked cottages
and broken beer crates, fill the sagging apron and
stagger back to their narrow, cavernous passage-ways,
wiping the weary head and disappear.

Trundle old legs, trundle. Somewhere a lone voice
calls.
TibbyTibbyTibbyTibbyTibbyTibbyTibby?
Fetch more wood for winter has come.
Fasten the window.   Poor Tibby is dead.
And where is Robin?
And where is
jacob
small?
is he there
at
all?

'Jackers?'
'Yes?'
'Do you love me?'
'No.'
'Do you love me?'
'I said, no.'
'Quit stallin'. I want a dyrect answer.'
'Jacob, I *don't* love you.'
'Why?'
'Because you're irresponsible, a failure, a has-been, a drunkard, and for all I know, a philanderer.'
(Creepers jeepers) 'That's a nice black bra you're wearing, very 'exy, quite in fashion. When I met you on the lawn at that Hawarden teaparty, I said to myself, now there's a *real* fashionplate.'
'How do you know they're in fashion?'
'Um um because you're wearing one.'
'Oh God, Jacob Small, I know you well, your mind's always in your trousers.'
Jacob goes to look out the window at the loving black and white night, but she has drawn the curtains. He thinks of the mountain, his big dawn-coloured horse,

slivers of ice tinkling on trees, the Southern Pacific Sea and the great white whale, and Katie's father and brothers ploughing.

'Do you know,' he says looking back from the window, 'I found an early copy of Melville's *Oomoo* in the shop this morning?'

'I don't give a damn about *Omo*, what about me, and what about Gideon?'

He stabs at his dinner. '*Oomoo*. Jolly nice chicken, love, it cuts just like butter.'

'It's veal.'

'Veal? Is it reely? Reely? It tastes just like chicken.'

She sniffs and snorts. 'Why are you home so early? What did you do today. To what do I owe this pleasure?'

(Our next question comes from Mrs F. Ing of Leeds who wants the Brains Trust to answer . . .) 'The crisis is over, love, it's over.'

'What crisis?'

'The, um, financial crisis.'

'Financial crisis. (Sniff sniff) You know as well as I, you couldn't even manage a piggy bank, let alone a bankrupt bookshop run by a senile old idiot in a bankrupt town.'

'Ha-ha piggy bank very funny ha-ha. Aw come on, Jackers, if I love you, you must love me.'

His wife looks at him, her fork poised over an attempt at Elizabeth David's art. 'Do you know what, Jacob?'

'You're mad and I'm not. What?'

'I wish to God I'd never married you.'

(Gawd) 'I had to go down to South Flagstaff this after-

noon. Very grim down there, very grim. Makes you think. (Puts on his earthquake look.) Very dismal and cold.' He stretches his nose. (There's nae luck about the house.) 'Plenty of people worse off than we are. We should be thankful, all snug and cosy.'
'Why are you home so early?'
'Don't you want me home?'
'How can I want you home if you're never home?'
'Well I *am* home.'
'You're never home.'
(What rhymes with home? Dome? Comb? Foam? Roam? Tome?)
'Well I *am* gnome.'
'Nome?'
'Gnome, Grumpy Gnome, Plastic Gnome, Concrete Gnome, Rubber Gnome, (life-size, male or female with realistic anatomical features, aaaah aaaah) Zurich Gnome.'
'What?'
'Nome is the capital of Alaska. All roads lead to Nome. Heh heh.'
'I wish to God I'd never married you.'
'Aw, Jackers, I gnome you've had a hard Rome to comb but you reely shouldn't groam now I'm chrome.'
'You think you're clever, don't you?'
'Now and again I'm a bit sparky. Space Chimp sparky. Great chicken, pet.'
'Why are you always so late home?' Sniff sniff.
'Um um, business business (heave sigh) look, Jackers, what about to bed, to bed to rest our head?'
'Do you know what I don't like about you, Jacob?'

(Shit) 'What?'
She points her fork straight at his breast. 'You think you're clever but you're a failure, a bloody failure.'
(Eccccccccccch a mind-snap) 'And do you know what? What I don't like about you, Jacqueline?'
'What?'
(All is lost this winter evening, all is lost) 'Your sniff. Your fucking sniff. Jesus you've sniffed six hundred bloody thousand sniffs. You want your antrems scraped.'
Her black bra rises. 'And do you know what I don't like about you . . . ?'
'Not scraped, sluiced, hosed out, scoured, dynamited, quarried, blasted, grouted, drilled, bored, they've got a special nose de-coking machine now. There was an article about it in last February's *Scientific American*. Apparently if all the tubes in your nose were laid end to end, they'd cover over four miles of ground, millions of micro-metres of nose. The human body's a wonderful thing.'
'. . . Your rudeness, lack of manners, capacity for filth, your total lack, your genius for failure.'
'How long have you suffered, Jackers? How long?' He does his Marion's-nose-is-red-and-raw look (dark, knotted nostrils and adenoids like bunches of grapes) 'How long have you sniffered? You never blow your nose properly, there must be a thousand tons of dried snot up those ramificatious passages, stalagtites of snot. Snot like bats' guano from a remote Pacific Island drying on trays. Gawd, if it ever came in for fertiliser, you'd be worth a fortune.'

'You failed filthy bastard.'
'You'll have to get it out. Essential. Chisels, picks, reamers, grouters, post-hole borers, pins, needles, bodkins, old biros, bent paper-clips, German-jack planes, Black & Decker drillers, Waterman's six carat gold nibs, Post Office pens, pine-needles, Gorman's pipe-reamer, you might have cancer of the sniffer, mad cells, Bertie-the-germs running berserk through your nasicular passages, gawd, you'd better consult witch-doctor Gorman, there's nothing he'd like better than a feel up your quivering nasal orifices.'
'You bloody filthy bastard.'
'Jimminy Cricket, I can see him now, his pic-a-bic poised, pipe clamped in teeth (through hole in face mask) poised for the first experimental exploration of your tender snout, come to think of it, Gorman has nasicular trouble, he sniffs, Jesus you'd be tremendous in bed together, real Perfumed Sniffer stuff, two sniffs on a single thread (ahem), the sound and honking fury of it.'
'You poor, disgusting, pathetic bloody failure, you're utterly filthy, why I married you God only knows . . .'
'Knows, nose, heh heh.'
'Look at you, look at me, dressed in rags because you can't earn enough, the baby crying with hunger, living in this slum . . .'
'Aw, come off it, Jackers.'
'It's true, you failed sod, it's true, what I am going to do I do not know.' Sniff sniff.
Suddenly he is tired and fearful (mammy mammy?) his shirt cuffs dripping in his congealed *cordon bleu*.

(Gloombum gloombum, dead sparrows, little fresh seeds in gunny sacks, a dead lamb trapped in the wire) 'I'm sorry, Jackers, I'm sorry.' He comes round to her side of the table and tries an erotic Hindu neck-bite. 'Me Irish tongue runs away wuth me.' (What'll I doo when yoo are far away, what'll I doo, what'll I doo, what'll I doo?)
'You filthy bastard.'
'Look look (kiss kiss) I'm a little bird hunting for seeds, (kiss kiss) I love yooo, I love yooo.' But outside, a warm, fateful wind is blowing and the snow is starting to melt, too late, too late. 'Look,' he says, 'Look look, we'll leave, we'll leave, we'll go north where the sun shines and warm children play, away from the windy packs of ice, to mangrove swamps and moist, temperate rain forests, Polynesian girls strumming ukeleles, crickets' songs, open air barbeques and sprawling, tidal, sandy harbours.'
But no one is listening and she has gone into the tiny, cold kitchen, the dirty dishes rattle and the budgie flutters beneath its little cover. Outside, the frail old trees rustle, and beyond the hills and far away, the Donahue brothers are ploughing and fresh white snow is falling. Another night nearer the grave, Jacob sighs, wonders about his fat wood pigeon, his dawn-coloured gelding, and the cormorant, and goes wearily to bed.

Up the wooden hill to bed for cheer,
Jacob's had a long, long day.

Bang, her dishes go,
bang, bang, bang.

16

Black rain, hard rain, it doth fall, sweeping from dark satanic hills, secret gloomy mountains and mysterious, high, tussocky places, where the blinded sheep is silent and the red deer has gone, long gone. The hard rain falls on growing trees and ruined chimney pots, on black slate roofs, on dodding bald heads, on cacti in rubber tyres, on cold jersey cows, knee-deep in rank, raw grass, on grinning gargoyles and country graveyards where headstones slump and stagger and fennel droops in earth of humus and fallen leaves by cypresses of dark. Where are the tiny flowers and tender shoots? Where is the seal and the giant albatross? And the spring snail creeping? Falls the rain, it falls on forgotten Jewish graveyards (Moses Louis Lazarus is risen from the dead), on Ionic crosses and blundering gasometers shooting sparks and breathing in the dark. In this rain, black Victorian angels fall with broken wings and lie in hidden places, where by day small boys play, where small boys play. The bird is gone, the bee is sleeping in the hive, and on the hill that keeps this place, rain is falling, crystal, crystal, on the helpless, upturned face.

The snow is stained with blood from underground drains, and labyrinthine sewers, dead leaves and birds' bones, drowned field mice and dead forest creatures, insects, gravel, chimney soot, coal dust and smoke sweeping over this country city. Now the clouds have gathered from battered peaks, the dark, windswept vapour blinding across Mount Flagstaff, Saddle Hill and Mount Cargill to settle on mossy roof tops, factory chimneys, the soaring shot tower, turreted embattlements and cracking crenellations.

Sheer walls of stone, the Gothic chimneys rise from patterned roofs of Spanish tiles. Jacob stands and shivers. No fires burning in the grate, no hot chestnuts this wet, winter day, the childish window seat is empty, no mother reading nursery rhymes, Tom, Tom has gone, and all the piper's sons where this rain falls on wooden villas and hedges of holly. Lead-lights gleam from ornamental towers and purple leaves fall from Japanese oaks on oriental pagodas.

McDermotts' Winter Sale. SEVENTYFIVE OVERCOATS SLASHED IN PRICE, the rain still falls and all is grey and gleams like cloudy broken glass in this winter light. MATRONS' COMFORT SHOES, the warehouse is empty, no more fresh, unopened stock for golden ladies, lying warm and breathless on linen sheets that dazzle in the shady, perfumed room. Now the ground is sodden beneath the boot and hungry seagulls fight upon the cenotaph and ruffled pigeons fly, burble burble, throbs the feathered throat as they peck at stony seeds and grit from trains that wheeze behind the billboards peeling in this rain. MOBILGAS FOR EXTRA POWER, Jacob goes.

He opens the shop door, creak creak, and steps inside. Today, as always, his second-hand world of poems, books and memories. Piglet is entirely surrounded by water, the Trespassers W. sign is disappearing, oh Christopher Robin, what shall I do? And where is Pooh? Where is Pooh? Books like terrible, hollow, mortared bricks, sealed with their messages, rack on rack, row on row, silent as the grave, no embrace. Where is Christopher Robin, and where is Pooh? Jacob in his patched winter coat looks at all the creaking shelves while their God and guardian, Aughatane, sleeps in his remote outback. He sleeps like some weathered tree, he sleeps. Vast vertical parapets of messages, tier upon tier, medievally stacked in spires (do you see the chaffinch?), silverfish and serpents, deckle-edged bereavement cards, quarter bindings, old music scores (pom, pom, pom, pom), Biggles, Algie, Ginger, gone, gone, gone, a terrible mountain of Marie Corelli, H. V. Morton, Scholem Asch, A. E. W. Mason and All Things Bright and Beautiful, the Book of Common Prayer, my little red Catechism, Sunday School Cards and pressed flowers my weeping mother gave me. Ho hum. Ho hum.

Now the odour of dogs and sheep, the movement of high-country cattle, piercing whistles and rattling river stones, Doomsbury appears from his rugged grave of rock and corrugated iron. 'Gooday, Mr Small.'
'Gooday, Mr Doomsbury,' says Jacob Small, 'gooday.'
Mr Doomsbury trails down the dark chasm of stacks and paper messages and opens the door, his strong old body bending and bowing before the windy winter season. 'Rain, Mr Small, rain.'
'Aye sir, aye sir, rain.'
Sermons in stones and Puck the Whistler, Alfred is the strong tree, a senior noble who once had his men, his flock which he led along the tricky, spiralling track on shifting slopes of scree; he knew the sound of the river, the rumble of wrenching stone, the smell of deserted mountains, the touch of the alpine flower.
'The rain is on the snow, Mr Doomsbury.'
'Aye boy, the rain is on the snow.'

And from the depths of his frosty, leatherbound volumes, Aughatane, like some Neptune of the great historic sea, is rising once again into Jacob's day. Doomsbury stands by the door, hovering between Sagittarius and Capricorn, dreaming of impossible snow drifts, the big river running, abandoned mine-shafts, sluices, races and Roaring Meg, his hobnail boots between the door and the street. Jacob watches this old hawk like a small sparrow.
'A long winter, Mr Doomsbury.'

Doomsbury says nothing, but peels his weather eye as the south wind blows.

Doo dee doo, doo dee day, the wind is blowing up your pipe and God is with you, Aughatane. He emerges into his domain, buttoning up his crotch and tying up his body with binder twine, spots of glue and bits of string. Black-booted and braces twisted, he stands like a prehistoric tree, ready for another day of books, birds and ice. The smell of home-made pies and gravy drifts in from George Street.
'Ech ech, Mr Small, you're early today.'
Jacob, heart cold and lost between cliffs of books and grinding icebergs does not reply, but thinks of hearth and home, of golden crumpets on forks, games of ludo by the fire, of hot milk and stories read in bed. Irish stew somewhere in the Octagon, Aughatane creaks into his mackinaw, pulls on his sou'wester hat, moves toward his colleague and they disappear into the dark and vacant street.

How odd of God. Jacob watches them off. How odd of God, then suddenly decides to try for a look in Aughie's room. Hum hum, an excellent opportunity to see what might be hidden there. Maps of gold mines and buried treasure, collections of rare books and early stamps, priceless antiques, hoards of old banknotes stuffed in the mattress, masterpieces of Victorian erotica. He moves down the passage, stops outside the door and runs his cold fingers up and down the panelling for secretly sprung catches, false partitions and hidden priest holes. No dice, he peers through the keyhole and tries the handle. The door opens and Jacob stares.

Brass bedstead, mottled low-boy, leafy jardinier, plaster bas relief wall plaque of galloping coach and horses, a mother and son swivel-bust, framed picture of setter dog 1904 complete with Canadian duck, deal writing desk, marble-top bedside table with enamel pitcher. Gawd, the Historic Places Trust should be notified immediately. Sherlock-like, Jacob slides open the morticed drawers of the roller-top deal desk and scans the contents:

Programme

RULE BRITANNIA—Solo by Mrs Teesdale
THE WAXWORKS—Sketch Monologue by
Mr T. Aughatane
THE LINCOLNSHIRE POACHER—by
Mrs P. Boonstead
OLD FATHER THAMES—by Mr T. Aughatane
GRAND FINALE—by Chorus

He roots through the drawers. Victorian condoms preserved in aspic? A miniature Japanese Feather Tickler? A map of an unknown gold mine at Mount Shotover. An 1892 Port Said Postcard? My Last Will & Testament? Otherwise: four million illustrated Biblecards, a box of paper collars, three post office pens with ink reservoirs, the cash receipt book of the Belleknowes Pipe & Brass Band Society, Unsolicited

Testimonial to Dr E. Z. Notman, Maker of the Miraculous Magnetic Nightcap:
> Dear Sir:
> I am pleased to say I feel in perfect health in every way since taking your last course of treatment. My head is quite clear, my memory has improved, I sleep well, I do not feel tired or sweat at night now . . .

'Hullo, Jacob.'

Aaaaaaaaaaarrrrrk. Cheryl McLennan is standing poised(?) by the door. 'Where did you get to the other night? I waited and waited . . .'

'Cheryl sweetheart, um um, look, sorry about that, I suddenly came over with nervous nightsweats, the result of great business strain, decisions, decisions, decisions.' He claps his hands to his head like Rodin's *The Thinker*.

'What are you doing in here anyway?'

'Tidying up for Mr A. There's a load of invaluable papers in here and I'm relied upon to keep it all in order. The Keeper of the Records you might say, ha ha.'

'What a lovely big bed.' She plumps upon the old handknitted covers and shows a good nine inches of thigh and crevassed suspender belt. Jacob slams the desk drawers shut and whisks an invisible duster over the inkwells. 'Look, Cheryl, love, (business man's ulcerated face) I've got an extremely heavy day . . .'

She crosses her wonderful thighs. 'Do you like me new mini?'

'Tremendous, tres chic, very high (sic) fashion.'

'It's a micro.'

He stares up her legs at her floral pants, then at her boobs. 'You've got a couple of mighty macros.'

'What?'

'Look, Cheryl, old man Aughatane might come back any moment.' But he considers this piece of young livestock, sired from the green, wooded lowland valleys (pants-pulling behind the shelter-shed, pashing in the tall grass after Sunday School, summer sweat, the smell of gymfrocks, tit-tickling and a free feel at the Saturday night flicks at the Masonic Hall, Jacob loves Cheryl, Jacob loves Cheryl haa, haa haa) 'What about I buy you a drink after work tonight, eh?'

'Aw, I know you, Jacob Small, you'll never turn up.'

'Of course I'll turn up.'

'Anyhow, I've got the morning off and I thought you might lend me another book.'

'My pleasure, what would you like?'

'Another with plenty of you-know-what.'

'You-know-what? Take your choice, love: *White Thighs, Twelve Chinks and a Woman, She Couldn't Get Enough, The Ultimate Pleasure, The Weird Breakfast, The Enormous Engine, Fun with Concrete*, you name it.'

'Have you got *Return to Peyton Place*?'

'Yeh, I think so.' He looks again at her bursting boughs and time has a stop. 'Don't you catch your death?'

'Nah, I'm always warm, you know that.'

His cold fingers close the door, and outside the spindly

trees scrape, against the slender glass, the start of another winter day. Where is Aughatane? He is far, far away. Post and rail fences, young heifers lowing in mellow grass, hidden creeks flowing, he comes and sits next to her upon the brass bed. 'How did you get the morning off?'
'Old man McDee's brother died and the shop's closed for half a day.'
'When's the funeral?'
'This morning, I suppose.'
Hum hum. Another senior townsman has passed on.
'That's where Aughie and Doomo have gone then?'
'I suppose. Do you think I'm a very naughty girl?'
Uuuuuuuuurrrrgh. Big leery grin. 'Naughty but nice.'
Pat pat juicy thigh. Pokes fingers for a moment under stocking top. What would life be without this little mountain creature?
'What a funny old bed. Is this where Mr Aughatane lives?'
'Yeh.'
She eases off the bedstead and, skirts on high, looks around the room. The Woodstock Rugby Representatives 1909 stare at her. 'What's this old thing?'
'A jardinier *circa* 1898.'
?
'Never mind. Look, I've got a little job to do, love.'
'What are you going to do?'
'Shut up the book emporium in this time of unbearable bereavement.'
'I never know what you're up to next.'

'You'll have the best morning off in your life. I'll get me rubber scuba suit and we'll silent-read *Pleasures With Plastic* together. Very droll, very kinky, heh heh.'
'Garn.' Arms akimbo, she watches him go.

He whips down the corridor and back into the shop. Dark emptiness and the sound of a million books. Jacob rats under the counter and finds a piece of cardboard and a Day-Glo pen.

> OWING TO A TRAGIC DEATH
> THIS SHOP IS CLOSED FROM
> 9.00 TO 12 NOON

He props up the notice in the window.

'Crikey, you weren't long, were you?'
He squints into the passage and closes Aughatane's door.
'Nup, swift as light and bright as a Colgate Smile.'
Tock tock, goes the old man's clock.
'Come on, Cheryl,' he says from the Birmingham bed, 'I've got a real beauty for you here: *The Secret Life of George Eliot, Being a Collection of the More Scandalous Writings of a Victorian Pornographer*.' She sits upside him and pokes herself out, tit, thigh and hip as the Black Country bedsprings rattle. 'When I entered her boudoir,' Jacob reads, 'I perceived that she was standing some distance from me, and upon my drawing near, she daintily raised her dress to reveal

the most superb pair of buttocks I had ever seen, smelling of rare spices and glistening with strange and intriguing oils from the East. Wickedly, this voluptuous lady of the night came toward me, her hand coyly placed upon this usually forbidden region, saying, "This evening, kind sir, I should like you to put it there . . ." '

'Oooooooh,' breathes Cheryl grabbing him tightly, 'ooooooh, ooooooh, ooooooh.'

Over the hills towards the bay, the mournful pipes are playing.

17

Black bag in hand, Gorman lumbers stealthily through the weeping willow trees, past the ornamental privet hedge and opens Mrs Miffawney's front gate.
'Good afternoon, Mr Small. They're digging up the road so I see.' Mrs Dolan squints at him through her pebble-lensed bifocals, then hammers home a gladioli stake through her sleeping bulbs. Gorman pauses uncertainly beneath the sombre marcacarpa. Mrs Dolan's hedgeplants quiver as she drills holes and tops them up with blood and bone. 'Mr Small? I'm ringing up the Corporation tomorrow. They've tramped all over me bulb beds laying them pipes.' Her face peers through the hole in the hedge. 'Mr Small?'

The opossum in the whiteywood tree regards them both with his wide and shining eye.
'Have you seen the paper boy, Mr Small? I'm going to ring the *Daily Times*.   Mr Small?'
Gorman stands motionless as she sniffs behind the hedge, trundles with her pots, tears up shoots by their

roots, then disappears from view. His cherrywood dead between his teeth, he moves again, down the path, past Jacob's fowl house, on to the creaking verandah and through the half-open front door.

Mrs Dolan watches him go inside, tears the head from a geranium and crumbles a knob of super-phosphate. 'Mrs Miffawney dear? Areyouthere?   Areyouthere?'

Inside the vast reception hall, Gorman blunders against the antique letter rack, trips on the patterned square of Axminster and groans up the winding stairs. Mrs Miffawney's kitchen door silently closes.
'Good Lord, Jacqueline,' Gorman intones, now safely ensconced on the sofa and digging for his equipment in his cavernous pockets, 'who is that woman next door?'
'Bitchface Dolan,' comes the sweet reply. 'Terrible old busybody. For some strange reason, Jacob's always talking to her about her wretched garden.'
'I didn't know he was interested in gardening.'
'Hah, he's interested in everything. Jack of all trades and master of none.'
Through clouds of smoke, Gorman looks at his mistress(?) as she comes toward him, her dressing gown half undone down her front. 'How (coff coff) are you keeping, Jacqueline dear?'
'Rotten, absolutely rotten. He's bloody impossible. We had a terrible row last night and I've never heard such filth in all my life. Dreadful obscenities (she

droops down beside him) you're my one comfort, Gorman dear.'

Gorman breaks a match with his surgical thumb and steals a look at her nipples gently popping through her bodice.

'Ah, ah, (shifting arm classically along back of couch) I'm not due at Preventive Medicine until three.'

'Good,' she sighs, letting her head fall upon his tweedy shoulder, 'do you think I sniff?'

'Sniff?'

'That bastard said I sniffed.'

'Jacqueline dear, all the time I've known you I've never heard you sniff.' He looks again at her breasts rising and falling, puts his pipe carefully back in his pocket and prepares his oration. 'As a matter of fact, Jacqueline, I do have some rather unpleasant news I think you should know about.'

She lifts her head and stares at him. 'What unpleasant news?'

'Well (huff heave puff) the other night I saw Jacob down at the Bowling Green Hotel with a young lady and (hurk hurk) they seemed to know each other very well.'

Gorman pauses pregnantly for the desired effect.

'Did you now?' Her blue eyes gleam. 'How did you know they knew each other well?'

Gorman warms to his subject. 'By what she was saying, ah ah, all kinds of innuendoes.'

'Really? Who was she?'

He clears his throat and poises. 'A girl called Cheryl McLennan who works at a barbers' shop.'

'What's she like?'
'Well, ah, she's overweight and a bit obvious with a reputation I'm told.'
'Aha,' she lets her head drop again, 'and he said I sniffed, coming home late night after night (she squeezes out a silent tear) stocktaking, financial trouble, that's a laugh, and me stuck up here, I've only got you now, haven't I, Gorman?' Sniff sniff.

His day's work done, Gorman closes his hand around her shoulder. 'I thought it only my duty to tell you, Jacqueline.'
'Thank you, Gorman. At least you think I'm nice, don't you?'
She undoes the belt of her dressing gown and stretches her torso, legs and toes. (Huff puff, excited inventory: sheer night-dress, décolleté with slender shoulder straps; breasts bubbing from lacy bodice; navel in flat belly; bikini briefs; thighs; legs; feet and toes wriggling.)
'Sooperb, my dear, sooperb.'
One tiny strap falls magically down her shoulder as he watches through bushy brows. 'I hope you aren't too upset but I felt I had to tell you.'
She lowers her left shoulder and the other strap falls. 'Of course I'm upset. I've wasted four years of my life in this dreadful hole. Why he stays here I'll never know, and now he's been carrying on behind my back.' She squeezes another tear and looks up at him. 'Gorman, I want you to comfort me.'
Gallons of blood pump through his tubes and he

places his hand on her belly. 'And I want you to kiss me . . .' He leans forward with lips ready, but she moves her hands to her breastlets and down to her bikini atoll. '. . . there, there, and there.'
'T***E?'
'Come on, Gorman dear,' she whispers, standing up and her nightdress coming down, 'bed's the best place you can comfort me.'
Aaaaaaaaaark, hey ho and up she rises, and he follows her through the door.

Side by side they lie in Jacob's double bed, she with her nightdress pulled above her waist and crumpled pants upon the floor. Gorman, stripped to his bulky buff, lies nervously staring at the ornate plaster ceiling. 'You're a married woman, Jacqueline, you know.'
'Of course I am, but that hasn't stopped you, has it? Anyway, what has our fine friend Jacob been doing with his little tart?'
'I know but (mumble mumble) you haven't got the time, have you? I seem to have mislaid my Rolex and I'm due at Preventive Medicine at . . .'
'Three. There's plenty of time. Make me a cup of tea before Gideon wakes up.'
'Why did you call him Gideon?'
'It was Jacob's mad idea.'
Gorman heaves up, leaves his guilty pleasure pit and searches for his jockeys. She stares at his bare bums gleaming in the gloom. 'You're not going to get fully dressed are you?'

'Well um ah.'
'Look, put on Jacob's dressing gown. It's hanging up behind the door.'
He searches. 'You haven't seen my pipe have you?'
She rises mermaid-like from the sheets. 'Forget about your bloody pipe and make me my cup of tea.'
Stuffed into Jacob's old boarding school dressing gown, he disappears.

Jacob's kitchen: a bone handled Swiss pocketknife, a yellow *Illustrated London News*, jam-jar of tadpoles, postcard of W. C. Fields, *Everybody's Personal Horoscope Star Guide*, a butterfly net. Gorman stands shivering and puzzled, trying to find the tea. Outside, upon the pole, the fat woodpigeon waits. From without, her thin voice calls. 'What on earth are you doing out there?'
His big body parts the dressing gown as he stands upon the cold congoleum. 'Shan't be a minute
          dear.'
Ziz, ziz.
Suddenly the back door opens and Mrs Miffawney's head telescopes in. 'Ah, there you are, Mr Small, I knocked twice but no one seemed to hear . . .'
Gaping bare and bollocky, Gorman stands clutching pot in hand, beard awry and gawking like a drain.
'Aaaaaaaaaaaarrrrrrgh, excuse me,' the head cries triumphantly and disappears.

'What are you doing out there?' the thin voice bleats, 'what are you doing out there?'

Genevieve, Saint, d. 512, patron saint of Paris, a nun said to have averted an attack of Attila on Paris. Feast Jan. 3.
Genhis Khan: see Jenghiz Khan.
Genissiat Dam, France: see Rhone.
genista: see Broom.
genitive: see Case.

Hum hum. Jacob shoves his *Columbia Viking* back in his raincoat pocket and stands looking at the magic lanterns wonderfully flickering in the dark. Ha ha, they're digging up the road so I see, he looks at the rubble and thinks of fossils, digging holes to China, backsliding down piles of scoria, navvies with cloth caps and ripe old pipes, little green houses on wheels and the charcoal brazier brightly burning. The garden is empty and the willow tree is still. 'Gooday, Mrs Dolan, gooday.' No reply.

Magic lanterns, Barney Google, Tyger, Tyger burning bright, the mansion looms like some Carpathian castle, bats and bones (ooh, ooh) somewhere a horse whinnies across the bleak black paddocks. Christopher Columbus, a step on his grave and he shivers. He goes down the path to inspect the hens, chick chick, scratch scratch, only the sound of a falling feather. From the gully, the smell of dusty smoke stacks and ti-tree fires, the inevitable bagpipes mourning Cullodon, the feel of the sub-temperate trees, dank creeper and rats sniffing in deserted cribs. Jacob pauses, picks his nose, looks toward Mount Cargill and wonders how best this life may be spent.

Away the bay and the twinkling lights. (Just like fairyland, aren't they, dear?) Under the moon, the southern sea is red with blood pouring from the stricken city.

I'm the sheik of Araby, nothing ever worries me,
            bum bum,
at night when you're asleep, into your bed I'll creep,
            bum bum.
Jacob Small's got no balls, Jacob Small's got no balls,
         once I dwelt in ivy halls.

Within the house, the smell of boiled broccoli, dead matches and burnt dripping. LAST ONE IN MUST LOCK THE DOOR. WHEN WET PLEASE REMOVE SHOES. NO TEA MAKING AFTER 9 P.M. Signs and portents of happier days. He breaks an arm off the indoor plant and makes his way up the stairs. But the kitchen door opens and a familiar voice calls. 'Excuse me, Mr Small, have you got a minute?'

Shake shake, shudder shudder, Flagstaff's wind starts to blow from the far-flung Lammerlaws.

Cuckolded by a medico, a parvenu Dr Findlay with a face like a pile-infected monkey's arse, *et tu* Jacob Small (are you there at all?). He slowly climbs the stairs, opens the door and finds her standing there (with her arse all bare, every little wriggle makes the boys all stare.) What to do? What to do? An early foggy morning duel with Gorman (top hats, capes, the trees at Robin's Nest silently dripping and Gorman's bearded bumface gaping as he sees his left nacker expertly removed by Jacob's invisible foil.) He stares at her gimlet-eyed and decides on his W. C. Fields laugh. 'Ha-haaaaaargh, ha-haaaaaargh.' Pause pause. 'So bloody old Gormo finally made it. The vaginal Valhalla. Ha-haaaaaaargh.' She stands. Why is she not shocked, weeping and repentant?

'Just a minute, I know what *you've* been doing, ladies' man.'

(Omygod. Press attack. Never give a sucker an even break.) 'Still waters run deep, eh? It's always the bloody clergyman's daughter . . .'

'I'm not a clergyman's daughter, you philandering sod.'

'. . . those from the straightlaced respectable, on-the-bended-knee, high country tea-on-the-lawn, coming-out-at-eighteen-I'm-still-a-virgin-families. Butter wouldn't melt in your mouth (uuuurgh) would it?'

'I *know* what you've been doing, you adulterer.'
'Still waters really run deep.'
'Listen, Jacob, I know *who* you've been doing while I've been stuck up here.'
(Holy Moses) 'Whom, it's whom, and Jesus you've been stuck all right.'
'You've been to bed with that little bitch at the barbers' shop, haven't you?'
'Barbers' shop? Barbers' shop? What barbers' shop?'
'That girl Cheryl McLennan, you bloody adulterer. Next to that, my little indiscretion with Gorman pales into insignificance.'
'Pales into insignificance? You and Gorman? What did he do? Run his knobby pipestem up and down your spine? Stuff his pipe for foreplay? Compare sniffs in the afterglow?'
'You crude bastard. Look, Jacob, I'm leaving you, leaving you.'
'Leaving? Leaving? You must be joking. Ah'll have thuh last dance wuth yooo, thuh last dance togethuh . . .'
'I'm sick and disgusted by your affairs.'
'What affairs?'
'I've learnt a lot about your activities around town.'
'*My* activities? What about *your* activities? Gorman coming round here and stuffing you when my back is turned. (Sob sob) It's the pot calling the kettle black.'
Ahem.
'*You're* calling the kettle black, you bloody sly unprincipled sexmaniac. What I've learnt about you.'
'Ha, your tightarsed ghoul-friends (very funny) have

been talking, eh? I don't give a tuppeny stuff who bangs you, you mealymouthed little twit. But bloody Gorman. Shit, he couldn't even get his cock into a jam-jar.'

'God, you're disgusting. Your habits are disgusting, your talk is disgusting and your morals are disgusting. You can't talk without mouthing obscenities. Filth.'

'Go on.'

'You're filth. Bloody filth.'

'Go on.'

'Your body and mind are like sewers.'

'Yours is like an ocean of shit.'

'There you are. Disgusting foul talk. You've been to university and all you can do is talk filth.'

'Oh Jesus, the university bit.'

'There you are. Blaspheming. You're common. Filthy common. The rubbish man is better than you.'

'I haven't met the rubbish man.'

'Don't be facetious you cleverdick.'

'Fractious.'

'Facetious.'

'Fractious, facetious, oi, oi.'

'Why I married you, I do not know.'

'Ha ha ha.'

'I must have been mad.'

'What's Gorman like? Has he got a big cock? Big hairy men often have small ones. I bet he looks a real dag with his dork coming out the side of his jockeys and his cherrywood puffing like the cement works. He's no doubt been tickling your ovaries for months.'

'God, you're loathsome. Such filth. If you must know, Gorman is better than you, and he has manners.'
'Manners? What did he do? Open your legs and say: "This is an excuse-me fuckstrot"?'
'I never realised how dirty and disgusting you really are.'
'I bet you had to work on him. He couldn't do it by himself. Did you use the side position for invalids and geriatric cases?'
'Dirt, filth and obscenities.'
'Christ, I bet it was marvellous when he got it in. All huff puff and pipe-steam.'
'If you must know, I slept with Gorman because I was lonely, utterly lonely.' Sniff. 'You're never home, philandering around this dreadful town. You're a failure. I never wanted to come here. You dragged me.'
'*Slept* with Gorman, *slept* with Gorman? Why don't you say, made love to, had intercourse with, let him fuck me, rooted, anything. Gawd, I bet he's a marvellous sleeper, he snores even when he's a-bloody-wake.'
'That little bitch at the barbers' shop. Fat ugly little whore. Harlot, prostitute. Man-after-man-after-man.'
'Cheryl's a nice kind girl. (Ahem) A bit heavy around the mount-of-olives.'
'You think you're funny, don't you? University wit. All sex and lavatories.'
'Sex is funny. Lavatories are funny.'
'What's funny about a lavatory?'

'It's a funny shape. Every time I go to the fluid-release room I have a real giggle.'
'You're perverted. An anal pervert.'
'Lavatory normal.'
'You shouldn't be here at all, you should be in a psychiatric ward. I feel sorry for you.'
'There's a lavatory in the New York Museum of Modern Art. Or is it the Guggenheim?'
'I feel really sorry for you.'
'Duchamp hung it there. Well, he can't have hung it, he must have put it. Great art.'
'Really sorry.'
'It caused a great sensation.'
'You poor devil.'
'Have you ever seen the back of a plumber's truck stacked high with limbless lavatories—cisternless, tankless lavatories? Very droll.'
'You poor, sick, perverted devil.'
'I'm going to write a play about amputated lavatories.'
'You write something about your own sick, disgusting perversions. That's your style.'
'Bloody funny, you could have a play with everyone wearing amputated lavatory suits. Real scream. Heh heh.'
'And all the time I've been stuck up here . . .'
'With glumbo Gormless.'
'. . . you've been taking your perverted pleasure with that fat little whore. Could I ask you a *personal* question, or maybe your sexually sick mind couldn't grasp it?'
'Go ahead, I'm all yours.'

'Where did you sleep with her?'
'I didn't *sleep* with her anywhere.'
'Have intercourse, you smart-alec swine.'
Gawd. The sheep and the lamb. 'On top of four million Pall Mall Filters. Very sexy. They roll round all over the place, make weird rustling noises, then you can have a handy fag to while away the afterglow. Tremendous . . .'
But she has gone through the bedroom door. Click, the rusty bolt is locked. Creak, creak of bedsprings. Silence.
Gloombum. Gloombum. All is undone. Heehaw. He heaves around the kitchen, heart pumping and bumping, drymouthed, rain pissing down outside, trees weeping, dunny old cloud right down low on Mount Cargill. He goes up to the door.
'Aw, come on, Jackers.'
Silence.
Fartarooskie. Buggerdamn. What is Home Without Mother? The cabbage steams and his tired gut rumbles.
'Aw, come on, Jackers, the cabbage (like my life) is boiling dry.'
Silence.
'The goldfish has died. The budgie's laid an egg.'
Silence.
He peers through the keyhole. All bolt and fluff.
'Let me in.'
(I hear music)
'Let me in.'
(Open up the dooah)

'Bejaysus, I'll bash the bloody thing down with me broad shoulders, burst in and rape you.'
Silence.
'I'll go out, get drunk and choke in me own vomit like Malcolm Lowry.' Grumble grumble. 'Look, the goddam cabbage is turning black, there's a silverfish in the *New Statesman*, THE WORLD IS ENDING.'
Silence.
Golly Moses. Crikey Dick.
'I'M GOING OUT NEVER TO RETURN.'
Silence.
'I'm going.'
Oh Gawd. He opens the door, slams it, stamps down the wormy staircase, into the hall, on to the step and out into the garden. Southerly wind full of ice. Colder than frogs' balls. Back on to the step, along the hall, up the stairs and through the door.
'Hey, Jackers, I'm back.   I'm back.'

19

THE ZIP AUTOMATIC FRYPAN
The New Cooking Marvel
It grills, fries, bakes, braizes, casseroles, stews
DEMONSTRATIONS NOW ON

Jacob stands glumly in Gilltrap's Department Store munching his free Saturday morning breakfast. Pikelets, scones, toasted buns, chips and chunks of hot potato. Like mountains, the womenfolk stand beside him, overcoats below their knees, watching the bubbles rise from the fat smoking in the pan.
'Oooooooooow just like in a Goodhousekeepingmag intit Daph?'
Jacob telescopes his arm between the broad backs and downs another pikelet. Chew chew. Not bad. Just like Mother used to make.
'We got one at the crib, Mavis. A greatbuy. So handy. Does anything. I do lovely eggs for Dad.' Honk honk, chump chaw. Snouts dribble as the smells waft on breezes cold.

Dear Mother, is it worth it? Jacob grabs a couple more

scones, shoves them in his pocket, jams his elbow in a childish open mouth and makes for the street. Suddenly he stops: Gorman in bulky-knit and half-mast tweed trews standing in the Underwear. Red-Indian-like, Jacob turns and stalks his victim through racks of jockeys, trays of socks and fronds of hanging ties. Ha ha, just this once God is on my side. Undetected and right up close, he stabs Gorman in the back with a cold, stiletto finger. 'This is a knife in my hand, I wouldn't move if I were you.'

Gorman gasps, drops his full pouch supports and looks around. Jacob withdraws the knife, cleans it on his trousers and slides it back into the sheath. 'Gooday, Gorms. Heh heh. (plasticmaccock) Long-time-no-see (pygmydwarfprick) what's fresh?'

'Aaah, hullo, Jacob.' He gazes uncertainly through his horn-rimmed glasses at the Haberdashery. 'Nothing much. Aaah, how's the book trade?'

Book trade? Book trade? What shall I do with him? 'Not bad, not bad. The asking-price of 1948 *London Opinions* has just gone up.'

'*London Opinions?*'

'Yeh. Want one? The March-of-that-year-issue has some marvellous immediate-post-war duggery. Young Patricia Roc before she made the scene. She used them later to full advantage in *The Wicked Lady*. Diaphanous coverings and dugs everywhere. You should know all about that.'

'What?'

'Diaphanous dugs. Have a piece of home-made scone?' He circumnavigates Gorman. Big hairy legs stuffed

into hand-knitted socks and global arse straining the seams of his tweeds. 'How many hairs have you got on your legs, Gorman?'
?
'Well, take one leg then.'
?
'An arm.'
?
'Jesus, you should know. You carry all that jungle around with you. Cabbage trees, creeper, tree-ferns, bush-lawyer, moss, lichen, the rare Aphelandra Tetragona, unknown Alpine flowers, all species of tussock . . .'
Gorman snatches a packet of jockeys. 'Look, Jacob, I'm in a bit of a hurry this morning.'
'. . . roses, thornbushes, Victorian greenhouses, a carefully cut and constructed maze, admission fee one shilling and a love-me-forever after dark in the cutty grass high upon the hill.' Jacob leans forward and speaks *sotto voce*. 'Which reminds me, had any good fuckarooskies lately?'
'Aaaaaah, aaaaaah (fishes in bulky-knit and brings out pipe, matches, pouch, wampum, wipes beard, sucks teeth, finds raspberry seed under left side of plate, probes for shreds of Hollandia Aromatic tobacco, stuffs pipe, lights match, sucks, puff puff, jug jug, wonders wonders, nervous leer) I, aah, had a bit of fun with a nurse the other night, look, some other time perhaps.'
Jacob moves in. 'Reely? Did you reely. Christ, you're a real dag, Gorms, a real dag. You med students have

a marvellous life. All test tubes and prod. Free supply of condoms, curettes, pipe-cleaners and vaginal scrapers, all manner of blessings.'

'It isn't quite like that.' Gorman raises his jockeys and looks for assistance.

Circumlocutory perambulations, fee fie fo fum, here is the bum of an Englishmun. 'What size are you buying, Gorman? Forty-eight at least. Gawd, you're putting it on. Mercator? Great circle azimuths? Oblique Hammer Elliptical Area Projections? Anus mundi. What's your diet these days?'

Gorman drops the packet back into the rack. 'Look, Jacob, I really must go.' Huuuuuuuuuuurk. Gorman gropes for his bearings and makes for the door. Jacob follows.

'Look, Gorms, I'm your oldest friend, but with an arse like that, beware of the carbos. Nuts and prunes, Arabian dates to clear the bowels, a single fragile lettuce leaf, carry your calorie counter at all times, next to your condoms on the old pigskin. It is pigskin, isn't it? Christ, after you that young nurse must have a hernia of the upper gonads. Tsk tsk.'

'Jacob, I really don't find you very funny today.'

'You don't? I know what you could use.'

'What?'

'A Pifco Massager. Takes the fat off anything including gravy. Free seven days home trial. Now if you'll just fill in this form . . .'

Gorman gazes up frenziedly at the Town Hall clock.

'I'll see you later, I'm due at Neuro-Surgical at eleven.'
'Do you get enough exercise with that study and all?'
'Quite sufficient.'
'What position do you use?'
'For what?'
'You must have a favourite. The inverse Roman rings, the cross-headed pike, the open chassée, the Flagstaff Special, the Mongolian Crab, the . . .'
Gorman looks at him open-mouthed. 'I haven't heard of any of those exercises.'
'. . . the coupling Wedgwood powder-blue figurines. You're a medical man, you must know all those positions.'
'I'm afraid I haven't heard of any of them.'
'Jesus, with blokes like you around I'll go into practice meself. What do you do for Shagger's Back? Jackers is an expert at exercises.'
The penny drops. 'Is she?' Puff puff. 'I didn't know that.'
'I'll say she is. She knows every position in the book. Stop her and try one.'
Hairy eyes rolling, Gorman spots a gap in the traffic and lurches into the road.
'Perambulator position,' Jacob calls after him, 'meals on wheels.' He watches Gorman in full flight. Round one, haw, haw, haw.

'Hullo, Jacob, you look sad.'
Katie. A day of surprises. She emerges from Gilltrap's

and he looks at her dark hair and river-blues, the firm body in winter overcoat held with large safetypin, brown brogues and old kit bag. Should I tell her? Should I not?
'Yus,' he says, looking at Gorman retreating, 'I'm having a bad time, it is out of joint, oh cursed spite.'
'What's up, Jacobean-legs?'
'Aw, um, aw, fambly troubles. Christ, I'm pleased to see you. Which way are you going?'
'Down the road a-piece to the Medical School, I've got a Saturdee morning shift.'
'Well, I shall follow ye.' And they fall into step along George Street.
'I've got to make a stop,' she says striding, 'at the Applied Science Museum.'
'What for?'
'A few notes for the stewds, the young physios-to-be.'
'Well,' he says, thinking of all the timeless mechanical exhibits, 'come on then.'

They walk in silence for some time along George Street Extension, then along Great King Street.
'What's up?' she says again, her scarf flying in the wind that smells of ice.
Jacob looks along the narrow, bricked infinity of Great King Street, the terrace houses dunny black and brown, their upstairs verandahs blocked in with cracking fibrolite and cheap window frames, the black iron fences enclosing lilliputian front gardens of dank flowerbeds and dead geraniums. Already, the young footballers are milling around Logan Park, running

and jumping at this distance like little striped butterflies. Thin, excited voices float down the street. Come on, the Mighty Midgets. Come on, Marist. Jacob stops for a moment watching the game from the other side of the road. The tiny muddy bodies heave and push in the scrum, legs kicking and club socks to their ankles. 'Look,' he says, 'the tenth grade, the Holy Romans versus the States. I hope the Holy Romans win, COME ON, MARIST. I told you. Fambly trouble. Jacqueline and Edna and Reggie and Uncle Albert, and his horse, and the farm, and the crops, and Brenda and Eileen, and the pigs, and Mrs Dolan, (what have I forgotten?) and the future of Woodstock and Boundary Road, and Gideon, and you might say, the whole future of the Smalls.'
'And Dennis.'
'And Dennis.'
'Um,' says Kate as the Italinate porticos of the Museum come into view, 'happy families are all alike, aren't they?'
Katus, I am a fake, an exhausted Houdini sinking to the bottom of the river in a chest wrapped in chains, a cardboard clown, an out-of-work actor, an old caretaker of a closed music hall. He looks mournfully at the sodden acres of Logan Park with its rows of skeletal poplars and sycamore trees, the empty band rotunda and the cracked concrete cricket pitch. The Museum steps. Kate mounts a couple and looks down at him. 'All is not well in your magic Faraway Tree?' My Faraway Tree, my family who live in a toadstool.

He stops in the main entrance. 'Can I play the machines for a bit?'
She takes his childish hand. 'You may.'

A beautiful, optimistic, ornate, Victorian museum, deserted save for a lone uniformed attendant sleeping on a chair. From the roof, like some strange immobile mobile, a model of Bleriot's Monoplane 1909, PIONEERS OF FLIGHT. They look at the glass cases. 'Look,' Jacob cries, breaking away, 'the Synphonium.' He sticks in a sixpenny piece and pulls the handle and the great spiked wheel revolves like his moonflat, creaking, musical world, da da-da-da da-da da da da, da da-da-da da-da da da da, Wilhem Tell, the brass sounds of the overture drift and echo, plunking and spinning forever around the columns and through the struts, wires and frets of flying machines that have never known eddying currents of air and impenetrable banks of puffing cloud. 'Ha ha,' says Jacob, softly tap-dancing down the linoleum, 'a good tune, a good tune.' Da da-da-da- da-da- da da da, he lands in front of his first machine, ROLLS ROYCE EAGLE VIII AERO ENGINE 1917 and presses the button. The worn parts stir into life. 'Crikey Dick Kate,' he calls, nose pressed against the glass, 'this was the one used in the Vickers Vimy Bomber, the big twelve-cylinder three hundred and sixty h.p. engine, crumbs, this brings back memories.'
'Jacob,' comes her soft voice beneath the overture, 'I know about your family in the Faraway Tree.'
'Look, Kate, here are some more.' THE MARINE

STEAM ENGINE, a surface-condensing, triple-expansion marine engine, fitted with Joy's valve gear, throttle valve, reversing arrangement and feed pumps. He pulls the lever and the whole antedeluvian apparatus moves spastically like old men's bones.
'Jacob, I am going away,' says her soft, insistent voice, 'I am going away.'
The Beam Steam Engine, the Double Acting Table Engine, the Gnome Engine. Outside through the high windows, he sees the strange, architectural trees crucified against the glass. Benzene Hexachloride Killed the Cockroach. Sulphanilamide Knocks Bacteria. Silence. Wilhem Tell has ended, now only the dying sounds of cranking shafts and the wind outside, and the wind outside.
'Jacob love, I know all about you, and I'm going away.'
PHYSIOLOGICAL OPTICS. Are you astigmatic?
DOMESTIC MODEL SECTION. A winding staircase.
Jacob, alone now, looks at a tiny Victorian staircase like the one he knows so well, its superbly constructed rails, grotesquely carved banisters and carpeted steps reaching for the sky of its glass case, but hanging in space, leading nowhere and stopping forever at its twentyfifth stair. He stands appalled and reads the inscription: Made by Albert Trapp of Woodstock and awarded a Silver Medal in the Flagstaff Inter-Colonial Juvenile Industrial Exhibition 1880.

'Katie, Katie,' Jacob calls desperately, 'there's some-

thing I want to tell you,' his frightened voice echoes, 'there's something I want to tell you.' He runs to look for her down lines of glass cases. 'Katie, Katie?'
But she has gone, she has gone away.
And the south wind blows.
And she has gone away.

20

This is our Lord's Day, and the Town Hall clock chimes its quarter hour from the town that lies below. The sound of bells from St Kevins, All Saints, St Peters, St Patricks and St Barnabas rings and swings across Flagstaff's bald, old hills and battered gullies, past the small, silent factories, through the brick chimneys of Flanagan's Brewery, down the terraces of Southey Street, along the narrow corridors of Great King Street and away over the beating South Pacific Sea.
Jacob is outside, listening to the bells and searching in the old, tangled garden for mushrooms and fairy toadstool rings which may have grown during the night. Alas, there are none, and he sadly sits beneath the willow tree. He hears a peastake snap. 'Gooday, Mrs Dolan, gooday.'
'Gooday, Mr Small, I'm a bit late with me pruning, the weather's been that bad it's got into me sinuses.' Honk honk from behind her blind. 'Poor old Dad's got it too.' She lays her hand on the old brass pump and coughs in clouds of Black Leaf 40. Bend the head

and let us spray. 'I hear you're having a spot of domestic trouble, Mr Small? Tsk tsk?'
Get foocked. 'Aw, it'll all blow over in a day or two.'
'Very unfortunate. Tsk tsk.'
'Yairs. Tsk tsk.'
'What are you going to do? Tsk tsk.'
Knock off his balls with a billiard cue. 'How are your Phlox Drummondi? Tsk tsk.'
'I'd have him up as co-re if I was you.'
Co-re? Tsk. 'If you've got any slips to spare I'll shove in a few to brighten up the chook-house.'
'Have him up as co-re, Mrs M says that too.'
Weeping willow, weep for me, he takes his life in his hands and goes inside.

'Gooday, pet.'
She is rummaging in the cupboards. Clothes, linen, knick-knacks, old hats, bric-a-brac.
'What's up, love?'
She straightens up, tasselled lamp shade in hand. 'I told you before, Jacob, I'm leaving, going away.'
'You must be joking, pet. Ha ha.'
'I am *not* joking, and don't call me pet.'
'You aren't taking that lamp shade, are you?'
'Why not?'
'It's mine. It's a genuine Bertie Wooster I got from McPhersons. Worth a fortune.'
'Jesus Christ, Jacob Small, you can stuff your bloody lamp shade.'
Crikey. Try withering sarcasm. 'And may I arsk to where you are going?'

'Up north away from this dreadful dump, somewhere I can be warm and comfortable and live decently, somewhere for Gideon.'
Growing panic in his pit. 'You're taking him too?'
'I can't leave him here with a whoremonger for a father.'
'I never sold a whore in my life. If I sold you, I'd be a whoremonger.'
'You know what I mean, smart-alec.'
'And may I arsk whom will look after you and treat you in the manner to which you are accustomed (to)?'
'*Un*accustomed. Gorman, a man who's going to be successful and constant, that's who.'
Dreadful palpitations. 'Now you *are* joking. Constant cunthooks. Gallstones Gorman, the revolving leather-patched lover, the randy Rudolph Vaselino, the bedpan on wheels, the hopeless hernia, the puffing billy with a pipe up his arse. If you take my son and heir, I'll have the police on to you. Adultery, licentious fornication with gasping Gorman as the co-re.'
'You wouldn't go near the police, I know you. They'd have you up for all those books you've been stealing all these years.'
'Jesus, when I see Gorman, I'll use his balls in a ping-pong match, I'll stuff his fucking pipe with used condoms and make him smoke it, I'll set fire to his bush, I'll . . .'
'There you are: filth. All you can do is to lapse into filth. Why don't you go down town to your little fat whore and leave me to pack in peace?' Sniff snuff.
'Right, I'll do that (this will fix her, stern soap-opera

face) I'll do that (grabs exercise books, school pencil box with sliding top, Swiss pocketknife, budgie cage) I'll do that, I'll do that.' Heehaw, heehaw, bang bang, down the Boldini staircase, past Mrs Miffawney's open door and out on to the porch, dump stuff, then up the stairs again for tasselled lamp, set of matching inkwells, stamp album, cigarette card collection and stuffed prayer humpy. 'I'll do that, I'll do just that...'
Monstrous bangings in the hall.
Slamming doors and wheezing grunts from outer space.
Sounds of shattering jardiniers.
Castors shriek from old oak table.
Tremendous crashings of breaking glass.
'Chooooook chook-chook-chook. Chooooook chook-chook-chook.'
Oh weeping willow, weep for me.

'You're not moving out are you, Mr Small?'
'Me Mrs M? Naw, I'm just going on a short bush-walking trip to the old Lammerlaws and back. Too much business, all work and no play, haven't had a holiday in years. Huntin' shootin' and fishin'.'
'Make sure you're paid up to the end of the month. Shocking immorality, I trust you're suing, he didn't have a stitch on, in fragrant delicto, and after all I've done, up and down those stairs, the law's on your side, get custody.'
The word of God has been spoken and a dry tear trickles down her map of New Zealand face. 'Make sure the place is clean and tidy and you're paid up, it's

little enough I get out of life, that poor baby, it's the young ones that suffer the sins of the parents.' He climbs back up the stairs. 'You just march into matrimony without a thought.'
More slamming doors and terrible concussions.
'The younger generation.'
Hollow thumpings from old tea chest.
'It never happened in my day.'
Wrenchings and grindings of splintered plywood.
'I've had my share of worry.'
Violent rattles from boxes of rock specimens.
'Not a thought for the future.'
Screechings from un-oiled wheels.
'No one has Faith any more.'
Jacob sighs and appears from behind the tea chest. 'You're a dear old thing, Mrs M. That's the basis of a good collection you've got there and I'll give you a few more: Values by the Man Who Sees, The Change of Life, Your Letters to Matron, That Old Navy Blue, Have We Forgotten How to Flirt? Quick Relief From Haemorrhoids (Piles), Beatnik Children Worry Parents. Your bowels are twisted and you're talking shit.'
'Ooooooooooooow.' Bang.

'You're not moving out are you, Mr Small?'
Christopher Columbus. 'Naw, Mrs D. The Chinese are coming through the Heads on paper rafts, millions of wily orientals, I'm making for the hills, get out your Berlitz book, cover up your asparrowgrass pit, hide old Dad, it's the torture of the peastake, the new order of

the market garden, the battle of ten thousand Phlox Drummondi, chicken chow mein bombs will fall from the sky, in short, Armageddon.'
'Eh?'
Mouldy Hoses, he goes round the back to get his handcart and pushes it up to the porch. A bowl of waxed fruit, an inlaid Italian walnut Canterbury whatnot, a pair of walrus tusks, a pair of Vyella Slumbernits, a beaded feather cushion, the *First Whisper of Love*, thump, thump, thump.
'This will bring her up with a round turn. I'll do just that. She'll come crawling.' Mummy mummy. He looks up at the open first floor window. 'Jackers,' he bawls, 'Jackers, I love you.' Snick, the catch is closed.

Up the winding path beneath the willow tree and out on to the road. Jacob Small and his handcart.
'Have you seen the paperboy, Mr Small?
The paperboy?'
He looks toward Mount Cargill for his dawn-coloured horse stamping and sneezing in the paddocks. No sign. Where is the farmer whistling over the hill? He looks again at the mountain and thinks of earth and mountain waters that heave and rustle, secret pinnacles that only the tired old eagle knows, water lilies, the frost upon the crop, ice in cracks breaking like small jewels nobody has ever seen, of the cold sea running. Here is Jacob under a willow tree. Where is Pooh? Where is Katie? Where is Jacqueline? Where is Gideon? And where am I?

As the rainclouds gather, he tries the lucky dip in his overcoat pocket.
1943 HUDSON TERRAPLANE
Come unto me all that travail and are heavy laden, and I will refresh you. (St Matt. xi. 28.)

21

Deep in chasms of Gilbert Frankau, Michael Arlen and Hodder yellow-backs, Jacob lies crucified on his truckle bed. Another morning in the southern world of the skua, the gannet and the kittyhawk, wheeling and soaring soundlessly over the purple sea, another morning of streaming seaweed and tired old bull-seals waiting to die on embattled monuments of ice. Monday, Moonday, he listens to the sounds of rats and mice (and all things nice?), the clop-clop of Flagstaff's milk horses, the rumble of the wagons and the chink-chink of the swingle-trees, and the mysterious whisperings and groanings of Aughatane's vast, primeval emporium. Frozen chunks grind in his cavities and Jacob raises himself to the mutter of old men talking about forgotten things, to the smell of elastic-sided boots and carbolic soap and morning stew. Dark darkness, cobwebs and spooks, Jacob rises, dreaming of porridge and pushers, burnt toast and cups of hot, strong tea. From the shadow of the parapets, Jacob confronts his colleagues as they bend over the pot, picking their teeth with their long fingernails and sucking their gums. 'Morning, Mr Aughatane, morning, Mr Doomsbury.' Perched on their stools like two black birds of death, the old men do not reply.

Jacob moves on toward the door and picks up the morning paper. *Flagstaff Daily Times*. Mon dieu et mon droit, he stands reading the news of his world. Preparations for the Flagstaff Cavalcade of Progress. Homemakers' Display in Agricultural Hall, the Royal Antedeluvian Order of Buffaloes Annual Conference, Big City Wedding.

> *Cheryl Elizabeth (City Ladies' Brass Band) only daughter of Mr and Mrs F. O. McLennan, was married yesterday to Wayne Frank (Signal Hill Brass Band) only son of Mr and Mrs W. C. Smethoon.*
>
> *The bride's princess-line gown of white hand-embroidered nylon over satin had a floating bodice with a boat neckline. A gathered panel fell into a chapel-length train from the dropped back waistline. A special feature was the bow at the back waistline which was of white self material with a pale blue rose in the centre. A circlet of mother-of-pearl, diamante and tulle petals with a drop-pearl over the forehead held her embroidered elbow-length veil. She carried a bouquet of white roses and stephonitis.*

He looks across the empty street and laughs a hollow haw, haw.

In the morning of the evening, Jacob Small walks the long, sprawling headland, where the pre-historic currents of the Southern Ocean flow. He stops and picks a wild flower in the wind that blows his trousers. An immense, black infinity of sky, where toward the broken, serrated land, a bellbird sings, clings and falls. To the northwest, the great mountain chain shines in the afternoon light, and in the foothills the stubble freezes, the hay is cut, the mowing and the ploughing is done, the cows are dry, the dogs asleep, the endless, spiralling high country tracks are deserted, the sea heaves and the season sighs and breaks. On the cliffs, the moss, the south-swept ti-tree and the sea flowers grow; over the rocks the beetle crawls homeward; solitary smoke rises and the sparrow sits upon the stone. In the lonesome, dripping fiordland, the mountain lake flutters, the reeds rustle and the water lilies go to sleep.

Jacob stoops, picks up a round, black stone, throws it and sees it fall into the sea, then turns back toward Flagstaff.
The south wind doth blow,
And we shall have snow.
What will Jacob do then,
Poor thing?

*Some more Australian Penguins
are described on the
following pages*

Barry Oakley

Let's Hear It for Prendergast

Prendergast is 'the tallest poet in the world'. A refugee from the dullness of commerce, he moves in on his old and unwilling school buddy Morley, who from then on follows at a discrete distance inspecting the wreckage as Prendergast goes from one fiasco to another.

But the world Prendergast is trying to inflame is made of asbestos— rock-solid Melbourne manages to resist all his guerilla attacks on conformity, censorship, Moomba and the Shrine of Remembrance, till he goes down in an explosive and spectacular climax.

Thomas Keneally

A Dutiful Daughter

'It is the duty of a good child to let his parents know the second they turn into animals...'

When Barbara Glover reached puberty, her parents suddenly assumed bodily forms so unnatural that they had to be kept from the world and tended like farm animals. Uncertain whether she or they caused the 'accident', she has found herself bound in dominance over them, impelled by a fierce love to organize them and her younger brother around the family's affliction.

A Dutiful Daughter is the act of an exceptional and provocative imagination, an authentic specimen of the new fiction which is not content merely to reproduce realities but insists on making them up.